Sideswiped

A Comedy

----------------Margo E. Peterson-------------

ISBN: 0692449817
ISBN13: 978-0692449813

A publication of Noisy Creek Press, USA

This is a work of fiction. Any similarity to events or locales or to any person, living or dead, or, is purely coincidence.

To My Mom

(With special thanks to the Hard-Nosed Zealots

for all of their advice, support and therapy.)

And to my students: driving is a tough, humbling learning process, and I know it takes

courage to stick with it. I learned as much from you as you learned from me, and I hope

you can appreciate the spirit in which my tale is told...and laugh along with me.

The Ten Commandments
Of Driving Instructors

Thou shalt not drive: suffer the student to drive, though thee be sore afraid.

Thou shalt have mercy on the students, and keep the commandments of the Driver's Guide.

Thou shalt not take the name of the Licensing Director nor the Lord in vain: shouting obscenities frightens the student and endangers thy life.

Remember the Sabbath, to rest and take tranquilizers.

Honor thy student's mother and father, beseeching them to practice with their child on the roads the Department of Transportation hath provided.

Thou shalt not kill thy student, even if thy student tries to kill thee.

Thou shalt not clutch the dashboard nor hide thine eyes—grab the wheel and hit the brake instead.

Thou shalt not hide the car keys, nor lose them, so the student can't drive.

Thou shalt not bear false witness by singing the praises of thy student's driving, when verily thee always wears "Depends™" on his or her drive days.

Thou shalt not covet thy neighbor's job nor thy neighbor's tremor-free hands. For only thou hast the coveted power to release our youth from bondage, and bestow upon them the freedom of the American road, to go forth in small gangs driving compacts that vibrate in rhythm, bearing cell phones, iPods™…Okay thou may covet thy neighbor's job, and take comfort that our youth are not lost, as long as their GPS is working.

•⁄•

Chapter 1

Glancing down at the dual brake, Sally made sure her foot was squarely over it, the "ready position" she'd been taught in instructor training. Hard to believe that had only been three and a half months ago—she was pretty sure she'd aged a lot more than that. Now she wondered again why she always seemed to schedule Mrs. Hanama first thing in the morning. So she could sleep through the ordeal? She took a sip of her latte, trying to focus as the car began to roll back.

Sally could have talked Mrs. Hanama through it once again. She could have said, "Now be sure to look back," and told her exactly when to start turning the wheel. But this was at least the sixth time. Surely it was time for the student to do this on her own. Mrs. Hanama backed out of the driveway, across the road, and once again failed to turn her wheels at all as she slammed her foot on the gas. They went airborne over the curb on the other side of the road. The back wheels came to rest on the sidewalk. Sally had stomped the cable brake, but it had failed to stop them before disaster struck.

They'd hit hard enough to knock the magnetic "Student Driver" sign off the back. Sally got out to replace it. This allowed her to curse without Mrs. Hanama hearing, a welcome relief. She adjusted her underpants and slacks. No matter how many times a day she pulled them out of all the wrong places, the car seat seemed to have magic fingers that poked them back in. She glanced around, hoping no one in this neighborhood of newish houses was peering at her from behind their mini blinds. That couldn't be good for business. Seeing her reflection in the back window, she finger-combed her bangs. The roots were wet with sweat. She tried to restore the shape to it by bouncing it a couple of times with her upturned palms, then walked around the passenger side.

"I don't turn enough?" Mrs. Hanama asked, as Sally got back in.

"No." Sally tried to keep any trace of impatience from her voice. "Remember I told you to 'steer fast, drive slow,' when you're backing around a corner like that?"

"Ahhh…yes, yes, yes,. Her student nodded as if she fully appreciated the wisdom of her instructor's advice.

But Sally had come to realize a few lessons ago that when Mrs. Hanama said, "Yes, yes, yes," Sally should be screaming "NO!NO!NO!" because the woman definitely did not understand, she was just being polite. Of course Sally only mentally screamed. To her students she always used her quiet, soothing driving instructor voice. This was one reason she was popular with the really difficult cases—people like Mrs. Hanama, who had lived in little foreign villages all their lives, and drove as if they had never seen a car, much less ridden in or God forbid, driven one. Sally silently wished God would forbid them from driving one. She could use a little favor from God once in a while, especially lately, with the divorce going so crappy and everything. Oh no, what was Mrs. Hanama doing now?

"Remember we have to be on the *other* side of the road, Murieta? See that yellow line?"

"Oh, yes, yes, yes…"

Oh, shit, shit, shit… Sally yanked the wheel to the right, and with her other hand shoved her clipboard down beside the seat, wanting both hands and legs free of any obstructions.

Mrs. Hanama giggled, then seemed to have a thought. "My daughter coming back from college this weekend."

"That's great, Murieta. *College. Sally dreamed forward to the day when she would go back to college. I'll get my degree, and be a real teacher, with a desk, and a whiteboard instead of a clipboard and…* "Will your daughter be able to practice with you while she's here?"

"Oh, I don't think she can. She saying she want me to practice with you more first."

"Ohhh…" Sally sank deeper in her seat. *Damn.* "Okay, now we're getting a little close to the—" Sally's head hit the ceiling as Mrs. Hanama cut the corner so sharply the tire dropped off the edge of the pavement into a deep pothole. "So that's why it's really important not to turn too early and cut the corner…But you're getting much better, that was the first time you did that today…" Sally smiled as she massaged her scalp. Checking the mirror, she saw a teenage boy in a pickup tailgating them.

"Oh, yes, yes, yes…"

"Uh—Murieta—I think we should try to pull over on the right, here, and let this guy arou—No! I didn't mean *turn* right—" the car veered precariously into a side road, swerving sharply into the left lane until Sally gripped the wheel and put them into the right lane with one swift move. She then glanced at the watch on her other wrist. "Well, I think it's time we'd better head back."

"We not driving on the freeway?"

"Oh, no…not today…we're out of time. We'll do that next time." *Over my dead body. And it probably will be.*

Sally dropped Mrs. Hanama near the mall. It wasn't much of a mall. Great flower shops, there and everywhere, though. Living in the heart of flower-growing country was a treat in some ways, but she missed living in a bigger town with all the choices that provided. She reminded herself again that it was a necessary sacrifice for the cheaper living expenses here. This was her chosen safe haven while she tried to wrestle a divorce from a husband who'd never made anything easy.

Her next appointment was, as Logan, her boss, had described it, "way the hell out in East Jesus." The lady who had called to make the appointment had said it would only take about ten minutes, but that's what they all said. If it took over ten minutes they had to pay a pickup fee.

Sally cruised up the highway, missed the turn before the bridge the first time, finally found the narrow dirt driveway after turning around, and was now bumping along from pothole to pothole peering through the thick fog that had settled into the farmlands around her. She squinted, trying to penetrate the grey film. *Windmill. Windmill.* The woman had said "just look for the windmill. Just turn there and Henry will be waiting by the milk house right behind it." The driveway seemed interminable, and though this area was thick with Dutch farmers, no windmill or silhouette of one revealed itself.

Fog like this was common to these low-lying flats, and had played a large part in the name of the town. When she had first moved here, she asked people where the name Mount Overlook came from. Everyone she had talked to seemed to think the mountain had been named for the beautiful scenic view it offered. But her research didn't bear that out. The town was definitely named for the mountain above it. It was named by English explorers who had traveled through the area in a dense fog. In their hurry to get back to the ship without getting lost, they had simply overlooked both the mountain and the river it overlooked, and hadn't noticed them until the next morning. Hence the name for the mountain and town. The Lookajams River had its own origin.

She turned around, thinking she'd taken the wrong drive, and headed back down the highway the way she'd come, looking for another driveway that might be the right one. Finding none, she returned to the first one and found herself deep in pothole déjà vu. Finally, as the fog began to thin, she rounded a curve, and spotted a miniature windmill on a mailbox. She turned into the driveway, cruised the muddy area between the barn and outbuildings, but didn't see Henry.

Wait! A tall silhouette appeared out of the fog. He walked toward the car, strained forward, apparently reading the sign on the side, then walked more briskly. *Yes!* She rolled down her window.

"I'm looking for Henry…"

Before she could finish, he explained. "Dad left—he thought you forgot. He said you were s'posed to be here at 10:30."

"Well, yes, but with the fog…"

"He went down to the Canary—you can prob'ly catch 'im there."

"The Canary?"

"The Canary Café, in town—Y'know, on Main…"

Of course, everybody knows the Canary… she racked her brain trying to remember if she'd ever seen this place. The town he talked about was like many others in this area—a collection of hardware and feed stores, a tractor dealership, and a few other necessities sprinkled throughout. There was a school, and a theatre in there somewhere. Surely she could stumble upon the local café. She definitely didn't want to seem hopelessly stupid after getting lost—she might lose the drive, and she could not afford that. *Well, Main is only a few blocks long, I'll run into it.* "Okay, sure, I'll try to catch up with him there," She began rolling up the window.

"He's really worried. Y'know, about the license…"

"I'll do my best."

"He's a good driver. I think those driver license people just got it in for old guys, y'know…"

"Yeah, sometimes they're a little rough at DOL, but they have a hard job…"

"Well, make sure he passes, okay?"

"If he's a good driver, he'll be all right."

As she backed out, her eyes fell upon the barn door. It was pretty smashed up. This was apparently where Henry had accidentally hit the gas instead of the brake. That's what Logan had said when he gave her the drive.

She headed for town and found the Canary. When she asked a waitress if she knew him. She pointed at an old guy in a plaid flannel shirt and jeans perched on a stool at the counter. "He's wearin' the red and blue shirt." He looked to be early sixties. His hair was mostly light brown, but he didn't look like a guy who dyed it.

"Hi, I'm Sally, I'll be your instructor today. She extended her hand, but he just looked at it. *I guess he doesn't shake hands with women?*

"I'm Henry." He fidgeted and smoothed his hair down. My car's out back,' he said then, grabbing his jacket, and glancing over his shoulder toward a group of old guys at the counter.

In hopes of sparing his ego, she tried to inconspicuously nod her head toward the window, to draw his attention to *her* car. She felt like Lassie. He finally picked up his cue.

"I gotta drive the car that says "Student Driver" on it?" He glanced toward the café window. His friends at the counter were nudging each other and snickering." He looked indignant.

"Sorry," she said. "That's the rule." She wasn't sorry. There was no way she was getting in a car without her own brake. Maybe after she took a look at how bad or good this guy was, but definitely not now. She needed to relax a little after Mrs. Hanama.

The car lurched forward and she could smell the brakes.

"Actually, Henry, it's best not to use both feet when you drive."

"What?"

"It's better not to brake with your left foot." She raised her voice, enunciating her words distinctly.

"Just a minute." He reached up to his ear and fiddled with his hearing aid. "Damn squawk box—'scuse my French—there. That's better."

"Now, just use your right foot for both pedals."

"Oh, no, no, I always drive like this. This is how Dad taught me. You can hit the brake faster when you need to."

"But it's hard on the brakes, because you may put pressure on both pedals at once, and also you may accidentally push harder on the accelerator when you don't mean to…"

"Oh, no…I never do that. That would be bad. Nope, I wouldn't do that."

She could hear the engine revving while they talked, even though they were now stopped.

"Do you hear the engine, Henry?"

"Don't sound too good. You should get it looked at. Could be yer lifters."

Try using yer lifters to get your foot off the gas. "Well, I understand you need to retake the test, and those people at the DOL don't want you to use both feet. You know how cranky they can be."

"Yeah, you got that right. I think they hate old people. They're just tryin' to take all our licenses away."

"Well, look, I'm just trying to help you here, you know? You have to play the game a little, just do it the way they want you to for the test, so you can keep your license, right?"

"Yeah, well, maybe…" He switched his right foot over to the brake. "Ain't very comf'terble…"

"You'll get used to it. Great! Then just put your left one over there on the dead pedal. Now let's enter the road when it's safe…" He glanced at the mirror, then hit the gas.

Simultaneously, she hit her brake and slapped the gearshift into neutral. She didn't want any more burning brakes. The engine revved as he slammed the gas pedal down.

"What the…?"

"I'm stopping you, Henry…" They watched as the car they'd nearly hit drove by.

"Jeez, where'd *he* come from? I checked the mirror."

"He was in your blind spot. I recommend not trusting your mirrors. You have to check your blind spot before you go. In fact, you can remember it by always thinking 'Signal, 1-2-3.' You signal, then check your rearview, side mirror, and blind spot. See? 1-2-3. She pointed. He scowled. She had a feeling he would have liked a guy for a driving instructor a lot better. But none of the guys in the office had the guts for these drives. They were all burnt out.

She had him practice pulling over and pulling away from the curb again and again. "Signal, 1-2-3," she would say. Henry would check the mirrors and pull blithely over, never turning his head a notch. She tried different techniques to get him to do it...pointing at the blind spot...tapping him on the shoulder to remind him...and visualizing. When she started visualizing hitting him in the head with a baseball bat, she decided it was time to stop. She got out, and walked around the car while he checked his mirrors, so he could see that she disappeared into the blind spots. That seemed to help a little, but this was going to be an uphill battle.

"So, ya think I'll do okay on the test?"

"I think we should do another lesson...it's up to you, but I'd recommend it. I mean, I can see that you have a lot of driving experience, and I'm sure you could drive circles around the DOL people on your tractor and everything, but right now, they're in charge, you know?"

He looked dubious, but made another appointment when she suggested that he might be able to use his own car for at least part of the time. "Remember, I'm not promising," she reminded him. "It depends on how well you drive." But she had a feeling he took it as a sure thing. Oh well. Maybe some magic would happen...a big divorce settlement? Then she wouldn't have to come back.

She picked up her next student at the alternative school. Fortunately these kids and the homeschoolers could drive early in the day which really helped fill out her schedule. With those and the adult lessons, she could get in a pretty full day. Not too full though. She always needed a break here and there.

Sally pulled up in front of the old school building. It had been an abandoned administrative building that was repurposed to the alternative school. They had done some refurbishing, but it could use some more. She switched to the passenger seat, and moments later a tall skinny boy in tight jeans slid into the driver's seat. With the back of his wrist, he brushed his long dark hair back, then flashed the permit he held in that hand.

"Okay, Stefan. Cellphone off?"

He nodded.

"Is that a new earring?"

"Yeah, and I just got my nose pierced this weekend. Do you like it?"

She never knew what to say to that. "The question is, do you?"

"Yeah, I like it a lot, and my girlfriend loves it."

"Then that's what really matters. "And what matters in today's drive is parallel parking, among other things.""

"So you don't like it?"

"I'm not really into piercings."

"Yeah, I noticed you don't have any. You should try it, you might like it."

Sally chuckled. "You should try parallel parking. You might like it."

"I already tried it with my dad."

"And how'd that go?"

"Not that good. My dad gets really pis—mad. You're usually a lot more patient."

"Well, we'll try to get you really good at it so you can impress your dad, okay? Take look at this." She drew a diagram on her clipboard, then got a matchbox car out of the door pocket.

"Then, see, when the car is at a 45 degree angle, kinda like a big pizza slice, that's when you crank it left."

"Got it."

"Let's go then, while it's all fresh in your mind. See that car across the street? We'll pull up next to it, about an arm's length from it."

"My arms or yours?"

"Uh-h, let's say yours." She hadn't counted on the literal interpretation.

He followed instructions, the park went perfectly, and they repeated it twice more. The last time he did it with no help at all from her.

"Wow, Mrs. Fender, you are an awesome teacher! I wish you taught at the school! I could definitely get an 'A' in math with you teaching it!"

Sally felt herself blush a little, and a warm satisfaction filled her. She was a good teacher. She would be a great high school teacher. But even in Driver's Ed, she was making a difference. True, it had its ups and downs, but at least she was teaching, and what she taught was important. Probably more important than English—she might even save some lives.

She was still glowing when the drive was over. With a break in her appointments, she headed for Costco. For one thing, she needed some tampons. She was due. Maybe that was why she had felt so edgy earlier. But mainly, she had to exchange the broken paper shredder she'd taken with her when she left that jerk she'd been married to. It wasn't broken when she took it, but it had stopped working the other day, and they'd only bought it about six months before—well, she thought it was only six months—so she should be able to exchange it. But she didn't have a receipt. And her Costco card had expired. It was only a couple weeks expired, but her glow began to fade.

Lots of people had told her that Costco was great about exchanges: no receipt, expired card, no big deal. But things didn't always work that way for her. Her body stiffened with tension as she rehearsed what she would say when she got to the front of the line at the Returns counter. She also rehearsed what the person at the counter would say in response, and it was always negative, and then her reply would be more impatient, and theirs would be snottier...so she was almost at the boiling point when she got up there.

"Do you have your receipt, ma'am?" The twentyish girl asked, when Sally had explained what she wanted.

"No, and I can't get it."

"We have to have the receipt, ma'am, it's our policy."

"I know lots of people who have exchanged things here without receipts."

"I don't know about that, ma'am, but I can't do it, it's our policy, you understand..."

"You don't understand," Sally explained reasonably. "My husband has it. We're going through a divorce. I emailed him about it, and he didn't respond. He didn't want me to take the shredder in the first place and now he's not going to give me the receipt. But obviously this was purchased at Costco. It says 'Costco' all over the box."

"Yes, I know, ma'am, but our policy is that because your card is expired, you have to have the receipt," the girl droned nasally. "You'll just have to try asking your husband for it."

"We don't speak."

"Well, ma'am, unpleasant as it is, you'll need to find a way to speak to him about this. I'm sure if you just call him up..."

Maybe it was the PMS, maybe it was thinking about her crazy-making almost-ex, maybe it was too many tense moments in driver's ed, but on the words "you'll need" something snapped. The tone of the clerk's voice combined with the gall of a little-over-half-her-age-know-it-all telling Sally what she needed, pushed her hormone levels through Costco's warehouse-high roof, and *"to the moon, Alice!"*

"We. Do. Not. Speak." Sally continued, using every ounce of control she could muster. "I would have to call my lawyer, and explain the situation to him—or more likely to his secretary, who would then relay the message to him. He would then probably have to call me for clarification, which is what lawyers are very big on, in case you don't know, just to *clarify* that for you. Next he would call my soon-to-be-ex's lawyer and explain the situation, and that arrogant little sleazeball would faithfully promise to 'call my ex immediately', and hang up. After he waited a satisfying amount of time, he would then perhaps, if it was my lucky day, and guess what, I'm not feeling especially lucky on this shredder-busted, Costco-infested day— he would phone my ex-to-be, explain the situation, and probably advise him that if he has any inkling of where it is, to throw the receipt in the nearest dumpster. Meanwhile, I need to get back to work. So you see, I JUST DON'T THINK CALLING MY HUSBAND WILL WORK ANY BETTER THAN THIS STUPID SHREDDER WORKS—DO YOU UNDERSTAND?" She enunciated. Or maybe spat, she didn't remember. Or maybe she shrieked it like her broken shredder.

Customers edged back from the counter. Unblinking, Little Miss Twentyish-Assistant-Manager, spoke. "Is there some shopping you could do for a few minutes ma'am, while I speak to the manager?"

Sally took a deep breath and headed for the office department where she found a nifty little shredder that was a lot more powerful—maybe even enough to shred a whole marriage (or a husband?), and cost only a little more than the other one. The manager overruled Little Miss T., and between the credit for the old shredder and the one credit card her ex hadn't put a block on, she purchased one fine little shreddin' machine.

Buoyed by her victory, Sally breezed out the door, humming a happy tune as she imagined shredding her ex's neckties in her new monster machine. *I'm taking charge. This is the new me.*

•/•

Oh shit, she slammed on the brakes as she saw the pedestrian right in front of her. *Double shit.* That tall man in the dark suit she'd nearly crippled for life was her lawyer. She opened her window, and he bent down to talk.

"I know things aren't going very well in the divorce, but do you really want to run me down?" He gave her a weak smile.

"Sorry." Sally gestured toward the front of the car smiling, shrugging—and rolling her eyes in a sort of Mary Tyler Moore way she hoped was charming and would indicate that she really wouldn't have actually run him down, "I guess I was just daydreaming about court next week. So, how does the case look, should I hope and pray?" She chuckled a little.

He hesitated a moment, then said, "You can pray...but don't hope."

Her face must have registered the shock she felt, because he laughed. "Just kidding—I guess I wanted to get you back."

"Oh." She forced herself to breathe.

"Actually, things might be looking up. I have a new strategy to discuss with you. Call and make an appointment. Gotta go." He waved and hurried away.

She rolled up her window. *Weird sense of humor, but he's supposed to be a smart lawyer. Well. I'm a good teacher, the divorce is looking better. Maybe this is a good day, after all. But I better get back to work so I can pay the bills, or they'll probably repossess my fancy new shredder.*

Her next students, a couple of high school girls, were waiting out front. Brittney, a blond with long wavy hair, volunteered to go first. Her friend Carly ducked into the back seat.

"So, Brittney, have you been working on your parallel parking?"

"Yeah totally, Mrs. Fender. You have the most awesome name for a driving instructor."

"Is that actually your real name?" Carly asked, her short dark hair bouncing as she shook her head, seemingly in disbelief.

"Yeah, like is there a Mr. Fender?"

Sally stiffened. "Not exactly. Let's focus on driving, girls."

A few minutes later, they were pulled up next to an old beater, and she was explaining the technique of parallel parking. She was grateful to people who left cars like this parked where she could use them. This one had been here for months, but she knew it would get moved sooner or later. They always did.

"...then, when we're at a forty-five degree angle, that's when you crank the wheel, okay?" She used the same diagram she'd drawn for Stefan. She smiled brightly at Brittney, hoping with all her heart that geometry would once again win the day.

"Okay." Brittney smiled back, nodding vigorously, the glare off her braces threatening to give Sally a migraine.

"Okay," Sally confirmed, still smiling as the girl shifted into reverse, then slammed the gas pedal down hard enough that though Sally hit her brake, the car jumped the curb, crossed the sidewalk and shot up the bank until they came to a stop at a precarious tilt.

"So…is that about a forty-five?" Brittney asked hopefully, after a moment of stunned silence.

"I think so," Sally said without thinking. She was busy remembering that was the second time today the brake hadn't done its job and she needed to tell Logan to have it checked, when she became aware that her cell phone was vibrating. It was the office. Given the situation at hand, she let it go to voice mail.

She took a deep breath. Carly, in back, had been speechless up to this point. Sally tried to muster a smile, and turned. "So…are we having fun yet?" She could hear a slight quaver in her voice, though she was usually good at fake bravado.

The girl gave her some kind of look, accompanied by what could possibly be described as a half-smile and a hand motion that might mean almost anything.

"Okay!" Sally said brightly. "Let's get this show on the road. Oh, by the way," she turned to Brittney, "Don't do that on the test." She laughed, but maybe a little too much. Both girls looked at her, then at each other, and she had a sense that they were going to report her to the Bureau of Insane Adults as soon as she released them from the car.

Now the office was texting. "Can u come by, ASAP?"

She directed Brittney back to the office. "You girls can go in and use the restroom—I just have to talk to Logan—uh—Mr. Nash for a minute, okay?" The girls were inside dashing for the restroom door before she finished her sentence.

"Listen, you know that crazy lady, Mrs. Hanama, that you've been doing lessons with?"

Sally tapped her forefinger on her chin and looked off into space, concentrating. "Hmm, let's see, Hanama…Hanama…was she short and dark, and driving off the edge of the road…"

"Yeah, very funny…anyway, she was in here a little bit ago, and she wanted an emergency lesson because her daughter is coming in tomorrow, and she wants to impress her. When she found out you weren't here, she tried to talk me into doing it. You know I've sworn off adult lessons—

especially foreigners, ever since that cruise down the sidewalk with—well, you know the details—"

"Yeah, yeah, I know, Logan."

"Anyway, look, I can take the two girls off your hands—they're pretty good drivers, right? Then you can hook up with Mrs. Hanama. She's across the street at the Asian grocery right now, but she'll be back, I guarantee you."

The girls came out, and Logan whisked them out the front door before Sally had a chance to agree, or object. She stuck her head out the door. "The cable brake needs adjusting!" she shouted futilely after the car as it pulled out, narrowly missing a truck.

•/•

Across the street, Mrs. Hanama carefully examined a piece of ginger root. She wanted the best one they had. She wanted dinner to be perfect for her daughter. Gina was doing so well—but then there was Robert. Mrs. Hanama's son worried her. He seemed aimless. He needed a woman who could steer him in the right direction. Sally seemed the obvious choice. Sally was a bit older, which wasn't necessarily a bad thing, but Mrs. Hanama had begun to worry about other possible defects. Why was Sally getting a divorce? She needed to watch and wait. A few minutes later, she scooped up her bag of groceries and headed for the driving school.

•/•

"Well Murieta, it looks like you've got the makings of a yummy meal there," Sally cooed as Mrs. Hanama came through the door, her arms full.

"I make special dinner for my daughter tomorrow," she said.

Sally peered into the bag "M-m-m, looks like good stuff."

"Maybe you can come?" Mrs. Hanama said.

"Oh, I don't know, Murieta, I'm not sure that would be professional—anyway, I understand you wanted a quick lesson again today?"

"Oh, yes, yes, yes." Mrs. Hanama nodded emphatically.

Sally spotted a box of tea in the bag. "Is that chamomile?"

"You like some?"

"Well, maybe just a cup before we drive…"

"Thank you, thank you for an extra drive. I have present for you." Mrs. Hanama reached into her purse, and pulled out a lotto ticket. "My friend at the store saying this is lucky, she sure. Like a tip, okay?"

"Uh, yeah, okay, I guess I could accept a tip. What the heck…" Sally stuck the ticket in her pocket, figuring it was probably a loser, but at least it would be a little false hope for a few golden hours.

The chamomile seemed to help. When Mrs. Hanama clipped the rose bush out by the back corner of the parking lot, Sally just said, "Now, Murieta, that's no way to do the pruning!" and they both laughed. She even found herself starting to believe in that dumb lotto ticket. Why shouldn't it be a winner? She had to get lucky sooner or later, and she was pretty sure she wasn't going to win anything in the divorce. They cruised along the narrow farm road Sally had chosen, thinking there wouldn't be any traffic there. The road wound along the river, and as Sally gazed out at the water flowing by, she felt almost peaceful.

"So Murieta, how long have you and Mr. Hanama been married?"

"Oh, we been together twenty-three years now. We have met in Canada when I'm being a nanny there. He's half Japanese, but I forgive him." Mrs. Hanama chuckled.

That didn't quite add up to Robert's age, but Sally decided not to ask.

"Japanese occupy the Philippines way back, you know."

"To tell you the truth, I'm kind of surprised you're from the Philippines, Murieta, You don't exactly look…"

My father—he's Chinese. We're pretty mixed up in the Philippines, you know."

This was nice, getting to know—*Oh my God!* Sally snapped back to reality to realize there was a hay truck coming toward them on the left. On the right, a bicyclist was apparently oblivious to the fact that a driver's ed car was coming. Mrs. Hanama seemed oblivious as well. She sped along, unaware that there was not room for the three vehicles together on that road, and someone was going in the river if changes were not made—now. Glad she had switched to Logan's usual car with the brake that worked, Sally slammed down the pedal, the car slowed, and the truck sped past them in time for her to grab the wheel and veer around the bike.

"Those kids on bikes." Mrs. Hanama shook her head and clucked her tongue.

"Next time though, Murieta, it would be good to brake, and let the truck pass," Sally instructed.

"Truck?" Mrs Hanama looked puzzled.

Sally decided she really didn't want to know whether Mrs. Hanama had actually not noticed the hay truck. They could work on noticing large objects coming toward them in another lesson.

"Well." Sally checked her watch. "Unfortunately, it looks like our time is up. We have to head back to the office."

"Oh, yes, yes, yes," Mrs. Hanama murmured.

Sally steadied the wheel and hummed quietly all the way back to the office. She reminded herself that this was a temporary job—just a stop along the way, a stepping stone. Then she remembered what her lawyer had said. She would call him in the morning and make an appointment to see what his new plan was. Maybe her new life was just around the bend, and wouldn't require an extra brake for survival.

Later, Sally sat at her desk in the little apartment that was home until she got her settlement. She looked at the box containing her new shredder, intending to open it and shred old photos and other mementos of her almost-ex. Then her eyes fell on the financial aid application she had picked up the week before. She intended to fill it out each night after work, but was always too tired and stressed out. But with her trophy shredder by her side, she felt empowered. She slid the application over and grabbed a pen. "Fender, Sarah," she wrote her official given name in the student name spaces. It looked pretty good. She could shred the past another night. Right now, she'd start filling out her future.

The next section made her stop and chew on her pen tip. *Shit. This could be a deal-breaker.*

•⁄•

Chapter 2

"*A* horrible driver? That doesn't sound like something—" Logan was saying into the phone. "No, ma'am, I didn't mean—it's just that our instructors are usually very sensitive to—yes, I'm sure your son was upset." He looked up as Sally came into the office.

"Like I said, I just don't think he would have—yes, I will certainly talk to him, and I will do all of your son's drives myself from now on. Mm-hmm. Goodbye."

Sally put the flowers she'd brought on the counter. "Her little boy is a perfect driver, and the instructor is a complete jerk?"

"Yeah, the kid told her Dave said he was a 'horrible driver' at the end of the drive, and now the kid never wants to get behind the wheel again.

"Have you talked to Dave?"

"Not yet, but the woman is a whack job. She's threatening to sue."

"Do you think she will?"

"I don't think so. I don't know. Shit, look around you. What's she gonna win? Where do people get the idea that Driver's Ed is a flipping gold mine? My guess is the kid *is* a horrible driver, but Dave didn't have to say so."

"And he probably didn't."

"And he probably didn't."

"And she probably won't sue."

"Maybe..." He glanced at the flowers. "Somebody die or...?"

Sally bit her lip for a moment as if concentrating on her task. She wasn't sure whether she wanted to tell Logan about the lotto ticket.

"No, kind of celebrating actually. My lawyer says he's got a new strategy. I love arranging flowers. It's so relaxing." Sally hoped his new strategy worked. After reading the instructions on the financial aid form thoroughly, she had realized she would have to include her almost-ex's income and all of their assets, even though she didn't have access to them. Her hopes of financial aid looked pretty dim.

"Yeah, well take a minute to relax. I see you're scheduled with that farmer this morning."

Sally took a deep breath and focused on the flower*s. God, imagine just playing with flowers all day. I wonder how much that pays. I mean, jeez, there are all these tulip farms around here. There must be jobs...yeah, that can't pay much. All else aside, at least this does pay pretty well.*

"Hey, are you gonna go pick that guy up? Logan's voice intruded on Sally's reverie. "They called yesterday because you were late. I tried to get you on your cell..."

"Yeah...yeah, I got your message later. My cell fell under the seat when I was going through some potholes." She stepped back to admire her work. The counter wasn't the ideal setting for her floral masterpiece. She was pretty sure they had gotten it from some used furniture place or possibly it had been left out on the street somewhere with a "Free" sign taped to it. Or maybe the sign had said "Free firewood." This thing really should have been burned a long time ago. Maybe she'd offer to paint it, at least. The office in general could use an interior decorator. It appeared to have been furnished from garage sales, or maybe from Logan's garage. And the carpet...

"So, Logan, do you think your landlord would spring for some paint and maybe carpet? I could do the painting, and look around for some better furniture for not much money."

"Paint, maybe, but you see the building...it must have been erected around 1970 or something. I don't guess he's going to put a lot of money into carpet or anything else. You notice we still have buckets in the back room, waiting for him to fix the roof."

"Yeah, okay, let's start with paint. And furniture?"

Logan shrugged. "Oh, by the way, I had Dave adjust that brake."

"Oh, thanks. A little too exciting for you?"

He looked sheepish.

"Anyway, I've gotta go. I don't want to have to hunt Henry down again." Sally headed out the door, clipboard and keys in hand.

❖

"So, you drove a duelie on the test?" Sally tried to wipe the incredulous look off her face as Henry stood proudly next to his enormous truck. He kicked some mud off one of the two right rear tires.

"Yah, that's what I drive all the time."

"Didn't you say you failed parallel parking?"

"Yah…"

"Let me guess: you put at least one wheel up on the curb."

"Yah, did you talk to that DOL guy or somethin'?"

"Henry, do you have any other car you could use, or could you maybe borrow one from your son?"

"Oh, yah, sure, I got the Pontiac. It's in the shop right now. Usually the wife drives it, but…"

"So, while it's in the shop, have the mechanic check everything out and make sure it's safe and legal for the test."

"Ya think it'd help to drive somethin' else?" He looked fondly at his truck.

"I really think it would. Today we'll use my car. Then maybe next time we can practice in the Pontiac."

"If there is a next time."

"If there is a next time." Sally walked around to the passenger side and got in. Henry grudgingly got in the driver's side and began wrestling with the shoulder harness.

"Ya mind if I put this strap behind me? These things are so danged uncomf'terble."

"Actually, I do mind. It's illegal."

"Aw, how's anybody gonna know?"

"I will, when your head goes through the windshield."

"Aw come on, we're not gonna crash with me behind the wheel."

Sally held her tongue, pointed at the belt, and scowling, he put it on.

"So, before you pull out, remember that habit we were practicing yesterday—you know, 'Signal…'" She nodded her head, prompting him to finish.

He signaled. "Where we goin'?" He checked the mirrors and started to pull out.

She hit the brake. "Remember Signal 1-2-3?"

"Oh yah, yah…" He gave a half-hearted glance out the window. "Oats're startin' ta sprout." He gazed out at the field as they headed straight at a tractor parked at the edge of the driveway.

Sally gave the wheel just enough of a tug to change their trajectory, avoiding the tractor. "Henry…" She pointed.

He looked. "I know it's there. It's my tractor. Ya think I'm gonna hit my own tractor? Sheesh." He shook his head. She was clearly nuts in his eyes.

They drove along the highway toward town. "Boy, the Lookajams is kinda high," Henry observed. "You know how they named that, doncha?"

"Yes, actually, I did some research."

That didn't stop Henry from explaining, though. "Way back when, them explorers that came here crossed the river without even knowing it. They were on their way back to their ship anchored out in the Sound," Henry jerked his head toward the water, in case she didn't know where the Sound was. "Yeah, I guess the river had a couple huge log jams on it then—big enough that they were more like land bridges—had trees growin' out of 'em and everything. Ships couldn't pass. Our city fathers spent years pullin' 'em out. They asked the dang government to help, but a'course they're never there when you need 'em."

Sally jumped in. "Didn't the explorers camp for the night, and notice both the mountain and river the next day, when the fog had cleared?"

"Yep. I guess you did do some reading, little lady. Boy, that sun…" Henry squinted and reached for the visor. He seemed to forget momentarily that he was behind the wheel as he fiddled with it, trying to turn it to cover the side window. They drifted ever closer to the drainage ditch at the edge of the road. It was at least six feet deep. Sally idly wondered how long it would be before he awoke to the danger. As she sometimes did to amuse herself, she decided to wait until the last possible moment before intervening—maybe a little scare would do him good.

Because the visor was blocking his view out the side, Henry didn't immediately see the cement truck that was coming around them on that side. Between the "Driver's Ed" sign on the back and the fact that they were now going about half the speed limit because Henry had let up on the gas while he was busy adjusting, the truck driver had gotten impatient.

Sally should have been aware of this, but she had her eye on the ditch, and was about to reach for the wheel when the heat of the sun on the cold windshield caused the suction cup which held her rearview mirror up to let go. The mirror hit the dash, then bounced into her lap.

Henry heard the mirror hit, looked over and saw that they were headed for the ditch. He overcorrected just enough to alarm the truck driver, who leaned on the horn, scaring the crap out of Henry, who then overcorrected back toward the ditch. To add to the excitement, a car now appeared around the bend and was coming head-on toward the cement truck. Sally slapped the gearshift into neutral, hit her brake hard and held the wheel tight to keep Henry from turning it. She thanked God that the brake had been fixed. The cement truck moved in front of them. The car passed, with the driver staring at them, apparently to see what kind of lousy driving instructor this was. Sally's heart slowed down.

Henry drove in silence for a few moments. "...anyway, then they met the Nookachamps Indians."

"And they thought the Chief said 'look at jams,' and since the jams were pretty impressive, they shortened it to 'Lookajams' to name the river, right?"

"Most people just think it's an Indian name," he said, apparently wanting the last word.

"And it is, sort of..." She wouldn't give it to him.

They drove along, both squinting at the glare from the river. "Jeez, what was wrong with the brakes anyway?" Henry said. Sally saw beads of sweat on his neck and forehead.

"I think the reason your brake wasn't working is that you froze on the gas at the same time. That's why I hit neutral."

Henry moved his left foot to the dead pedal. "So can you drop me at the Canary after the drive today? I'm s'posed ta meet the wife there for lunch. Buy ya a cup a coffee?"

"Yeah, sure," she said.

"I really need my license, ya know."

"I know."

"Ya think I'll be okay?"

"Will you promise to do all your headchecks today...no trusting the mirrors?"

"You got it."

"All right, let's get to work."

.*.

When Sally walked into the office the next day Logan was on the phone as usual. She set the box she was carrying on the counter.

"A light pole? Well, certainly, I can imagine how upset she would be. I'm so sorry. Yes, yes, I agree…" Logan rolled his eyes and pointed to the phone.

"I'll talk to the driver, I'm sure he had a reason…my drivers are well trained to make these judgment calls…uh hunh. Sure, sure—I'll talk to him and get back to you later today, or tomorrow at the latest."

Sally grinned at him, as she set her clipboard on the counter.

He hung up. "How was the drive with Henry? Any better than yesterday's?"

"Actually, he slipped in the barn and either sprained or broke his ankle, they're not sure yet, so he's temporarily out of commission. I decided to go by DOL and get those Driver's Guides you wanted for the new class. Do I get paid for the time?"

"Yeah, yeah, sure." Logan wrote something on a notepad, his mind clearly elsewhere.

"And you'll give me a $500 bonus for being so thoughtful?"

"I'm not that distracted," he said, still writing.

"Okay, then, I've waited as long as I can, what is this about a light pole?"

"You didn't notice the pole by the driveway into the parking lot?"

"No, what about it?"

"Take a good look on your way out. It's leaning a bit. Apparently Dave's drive yesterday was really nervous and hit the gas instead of the brake on the way in."

"Dave's brake didn't work?"

"She wasn't with Dave. Her father was bringing her to the drive when it happened."

"But we didn't do anything wrong then, why…"

"The dad wasn't sure the girl should have even done the drive at that point, but there was another student driving before her so Dave had told this dad he would see how she felt when it was her turn. He said if he had her drive at all, he would take it easy, under the circumstances, and probably just stay in the parking lot. But he went ahead and did the drive, and took her out on the highway, even though she was a nervous wreck, it was her first drive with us, and she'd only been behind the wheel once before."

"Ooh, bad choice, Dave."

"The girl was completely traumatized, and the father is furious."

"Have you talked to Dave?"

"He said she needed to 'get back on the horse.'"

"Or the light pole…as the case may be." She couldn't stifle her laugh.

"Thanks for the sympathy." Logan threw up his hands. "I'll probably get sued for the psychological damage done, go bankrupt, and you'll be out of a job, by the way."

"Maybe you can get a two-fer from the lawyer and get both the 'horrible driver' case and this, for one low price." She was laughing harder now. It was such a relief to see someone else having legal trouble.

Logan couldn't help joining in, at least briefly. "It's not *that* funny," he said as she held her sides, and tried to stop laughing.

"So, what about Dave?" She'd regained her composure, and was now worrying about the reality of the situation. She still needed the job, whether she exactly wanted it or not.

"I don't know, what do you do with Dave? I had already talked to him when I saw the light pole, just to see if he knew anything about it. So I was sure I'd be hearing from the dad sometime today. But Dave seemed to think everything was fine."

"She drove okay?"

"Yeah, according to him, she did pretty well." He handed her a clipboard. "Here's the drive sheet."

"He passed her?"

"Yeah, he felt she was ready to move on to the next drive."

"No notes in the 'comments' section…"

"No notes. Maybe he thought it would be funny for the next driver to get her without any idea of what had happened, I don't know."

"Yeah, and I could have been the next driver."

"He definitely should have made some notes. I told him next time he's in, he should write something on the sheet. But, you know, otherwise, it's hard—I can't be second-guessing my drivers' judgment—I wasn't there, as Dave pointed out. Everybody has to make judgments out on the road. And by the way, you are the next driver, so it's a good thing we're having this conversation."

"I had a feeling. But what are you going to do about Dave, really? You need to do something."

"He's my brother. He's a good mechanic—I don't know how I'd keep the cars running without him. And you know how long it takes to hire and train an instructor."

"So, nothing?"

"I'll talk to him again."

Sally spent Saturday morning shopping the thrift stores. At one of her favorites, she spotted a desk across the room that she thought would be a serious improvement over the old beast Logan had. There was some guy sitting in the chair, though. He had his back to her, and his feet up on the desk. *Damn, who's that guy, and why is he putting scratches in my desktop? The back of his head looked vaguely familiar...greased-down hair...and on the feet, those cowboy...or rather that cowboy boot...the other foot wrapped...*As she came around his right side, she knew—

"Henry! How's the ankle?"

He grunted. "It's good. Just thought I'd put it up for a minute."

"I didn't know you shopped the thrift stores—maybe we've got more in common than I thought."

"Thrift store? I'd call it a junkyard. I'm just waitin' for the wife. She's around here somewhere tryin' ta buy up every so-called 'antique' in the place. We could get better stuff at Walmart—cheaper, too."

"You seem pretty grumpy, Henry. Are you going to be ready to get out and go driving again soon?"

"I hope so. It's gettin' better, but still a little stiff. "

"Well, I'm sure she'll get you home soon and you can relax and get healed up."

"Naw, next she's gotta drag me over ta the bulb farm and get some tulips. She always orders 'em early cuz she wants some certain special ones. An' it's friends of ours so it'll take a while. The women gotta gab, ya know."

Sally's heart quickened. *Being Henry's driving instructor hasn't always been fun, but Things Happen For A Reason, as people are always saying... though so often it's a stupid reason, and everything turns out just horrible, not for the best like they pretend. I guess it's just a way to say, 'well there*

*isn't a damn thing I can do about it, I might as well say it's for the best.'
But maybe, just maybe Henry's a godsend after all...*

"You know someone who owns a bulb farm?" She looked hopefully at Henry, who was deeply involved in trying to scratch under the bandage on his ankle.

"Sure, sure, us old farmers gotta stick together, ya know."

"Do they need people? I mean, not in the fields, but do they have, maybe, a little flower shop?"

"Oh, they got a little flower shop, I guess, I don't know, I could ask I s'pose. You know somebody who's innarested?"

"Well, yes, I—uh—enjoy working with flowers, and I'm really pretty good at it, I think."

"You're not thinking about getting out of the driving business? I got some more lessons I paid for, ya know..."

"Oh no, no, no, no..." she said at least one too many "no's" and laughed a couple too many ha-ha's. She didn't want him telling Logan she might be quitting. "I was just thinking maybe on weekends or something."

"They don't pay you enough there? I could talk to that Logan guy. I mean I gotta admit it, you do a pretty good job sometimes..."

"Well, thanks, but really, that's not necessary. If you could talk to your friend about the flower arranging thing though, I'd appreciate it."

"Yeah, sure, I'll have the wife talk to Arlene about it, that's the lady of the house, she'd know if they need anybody."

Sally stopped by the grocery store on the way home and bought herself an assortment of flowers to practice on. She stood at the kitchen counter in her little apartment, humming as she snipped stems, and gently slid the flowers into place. As she stepped back to admire her work, she was pretty sure life had taken a turn for the better. She envisioned herself divorced at last and in college, working in a flower shop part time for extra money, and for the sheer enjoyment. Happiness would be in bloom just around the corner, even if she had to get there in a driver's ed car.

.*.

Sally was waiting in the car out in front of the office when Mrs. Hanama's husband dropped her off.

"Murieta…you look lovely today," Sally said as Mrs. Hanama got in, wearing a dress with big tropical flowers splashed all over it.

"My daughter bring it to me. She's knowing I love flowers."

"Oh, I do too. I'd love to have a job arranging flowers."

"I do that for a while, for my cousin. She haves a flower shop."

Oh my God. Another one. Maybe I can do two flower jobs. Surely I'll get one of them anyway. My luck has finally changed. Mrs. Hanama has to be so grateful to me for all my patience, she'll convince her cousin, and things'll be coming up roses in no time, literally. Sally was so excited she could barely get the words out. "Is she looking for any help? Could you put in a good word for me, if I applied?"

Mrs. Hanama's look darkened. "Oh, no, no, no…" She shook her head slowly, gravely. "She mad at me."

"Oh, that's too bad, but Murieta, you're cousins, I'm sure she'll get over whatever it is."

"Oh, no, no, no…You know that lotto ticket I gave you…that one s'posed to be hers. She pick all her luckiest numbers. I got another one for you, but I get them mixed up."

"Oh." Sally's heart fell.

"When I tell her what happen, she says if that one is winning, she won't speak to me again. I ruin her life. She could be rich and quit work." Tears welled up in Mrs. Hanama's eyes.

"But Murieta, the winning numbers haven't even been announced yet. Sally reached over and patted the older woman's shoulder. "Listen, with my luck, the ticket's a total loser anyway…"

This didn't seem to comfort Mrs. Hanama.

"Murieta, why don't I just give it back to you? I honestly doubt it will win, but if it's that important to your cousin…"

"Oh, no, no, I give you as a present."

Sally dug in her purse. "I must have left it at home. I'll bring it to you on our next drive."

"You sure?" A look of relief crept into Mrs. Hanama's eyes.

Sally nodded.

"Thanks." Mrs. Hanama smiled, then looked dark again. "She haves her kids working there now, though. She don't looking for more people."

"Oh, the job? Sure, sure, I just thought I'd ask."

The real meaning of what Sally had said about the job now seemed to hit Mrs. Hanama.

"You quitting? You not giving lessons anymore?" She seemed small and afraid, a child holding a giant steering wheel.

"Relax, Murieta, I'm not going anywhere," Sally laid a hand on Mrs. Hanama's shoulder. "I was just thinking about maybe a few hours on weekends, that's all," She hoped she'd get Mrs. Hanama's lessons finished before she found another job. Then she silently vowed to somehow finish her lessons either way.

"Cheer up, let's practice some parking, try some new things."

"Parallel parking?" Mrs. Hanama asked hopefully. "And can we go on the freeway?"

"Uhh…yes…we could probably start with parallel parking between the cones in our parking lot, and then we'll see how it goes, okay?" Sally pinned on a smile, hoping looked sincere. They drove around back to the parking lot, scraping the curb as they turned into the driveway.

"So, we'll pretend the front two plastic poles are the front car and the back two are the back car…"

Mrs. Hanama looked puzzled. "Oh, yes, yes, yes," she said, eyeing the poles.

"Here, let me show you," Sally took out a pair of matchbox cars, and moving them on a diagram on her clipboard, demonstrated parallel parking. "Roll back to here, then all the way right until you're at this angle, then all the way left," Sally air-steered furiously left. "See?" She smiled brightly.

Mrs. Hanama smiled, too, and nodded vigorously.

Sally had been letting her right foot rest on the floor while they sat and talked. The emergency brake had been on, anyway. Now Mrs. Hanama shifted, and turned around to begin backing. She had shifted into drive, however, and left the e-brake on. When the car didn't immediately respond, she floored it, overrode the e-brake and they shot forward. Sally got her foot on the dual brake and stopped them about a foot before the side of the building. Whiffing a burning smell, she made a note to have Logan tell Dave to check the e-brake.

They sat side by side staring at the wall. Sally took three deep breaths. Mrs. Hanama offered her a breath mint. She accepted silently. Maybe the mint would settle her churning stomach. She checked her watch.

"You know, this is probably a good time to go on the freeway—not too much traffic, you know?"

"Oh, yes, yes, yes."

Making sure the car was in reverse this time before letting up on her own brake, Sally still rode the pedal as they backed up, not trusting her student in this confined space. What had she been thinking? But my god, now they were headed for the freeway. Well, Mrs. Hanama always drove too fast. The freeway might just be her area of expertise…

Sally had to tell Mrs. Hanama to slow down several times on the way to the freeway, but she only had to grab the wheel twice. Once to keep her from jumping the curb and hitting a couple of pedestrians: Sally waved idiotically at them as they gave terror stricken looks toward the car. *Great advertising. Maybe I should stop and give them a business card.* And once to keep them from crossing the center line. She explained to her student that even though there wasn't anybody coming the other way, it was just good form, and also the law, to stay in your own lane. She felt calmer and calmer as they got closer to the freeway. She wondered what it meant.

She had intended to have Mrs. Hanama pull over just before they got to the on ramp so she could explain what they were going to do. *Yeah, look how much good that did when we parallel parked, or tried to.* She kept silent until the time came to turn on to the ramp.

"Here we go!" she said giddily. She almost added "Whe-e-e!" but decided that would be unprofessional.

They proceeded up the ramp at about 35 miles per hour. "Speed up, now, speed up, hit the gas, Murieta, you have to *speed up…* " She looked over at her student. Mrs. Hanama seemed in a daze, her hands tightly gripping the wheel, knuckles pure white, eyes straight forward in an expressionless face. To their left, cars whizzed by at seventy. Behind them, a line of cars developed and began honking.

"You have to hit the gas, Murieta," she urged again. Finally a response. Mrs. Hanama's leg moved. She hit the brake. The car behind them loomed suddenly larger in Sally's mirror, then backed off and went around, the horn honking, and a voice yelling "Get her off the road!"

"The *gas*, the other pedal, Murieta, *not the brake—*"

Mrs. Hanama moved her foot again, and accelerated.

They were back up to 35. "Faster now, faster, we have to go at least sixty. Hit the gas!"

Mrs. Hanama hit the brake.

Sally had to get her off the brake before they got rear ended. If she got her foot back on the gas, Sally could just push down on her leg to get them going. But she had a sinking feeling that would only be a temporary solution. She sensed that the minute she let up on the leg, Mrs. Hanama would hit the brake, and on and on *ad nauseum.* Since Sally was already feeling a bit nauseous, she took the coward's way out.

"We're just going to take a breather for a moment now," she said in her most soothing voice, as she took the wheel with her left hand and pulled them over into the breakdown lane.

When there was a very long gap in traffic, they pulled out again and with their hazard lights on slowly made their way to the next exit, which was mercifully close.

•/•

Later, Sally sat at her desk in the little apartment that was home until she got her settlement. She was enjoying her hard-won new shredder, slipping photos of her soon-to-be ex into its gaping mouth. She glanced up at the TV screen as the lotto numbers came on. The disputed lotto ticket lay on the desk in front of her. She couldn't resist checking it out.

Her eyes darted back and forth between the ticket and the screen. Her heart began to quicken as one by one the numbers matched up. Her jaw opened wider with each one. She imagined telling Mrs. Hanama that she had lost the ticket, then redeeming it herself and running away to some tropical paradise to live happily ever after. Or maybe she wouldn't run away. Maybe she and the cousin could just split the winnings. That would be plenty for Sally. All those hours with Mrs. Hanama would pay off, after all. Not that the woman would ever learn to drive, but by God, she sure knew how to buy a lotto ticket. *But the ticket hasn't even won yet. Better pay attention, Sal.*

Sally leaned over to set the photos of her almost-ex on the desk to pick up the ticket and fully savor the moment if it was indeed a winner. But somehow the corner of one of the photos caught the corner of the lotto ticket. She watched in horror as the almost-winning ticket slid off the edge of the desk and as though in slow motion was pulled down into the shredder with the photo of her almost-ex, his smile like the devil, seeming to laugh as it shook with the vibrations of the shredder.

Instinctively, her right foot slammed an imaginary brake to the floor. "No-o-o-o-o!" she shrieked. "Oh, yes, yes, yes," Mrs. Hanama's voice assured her in her head.

That was when she snapped out of it and sprang to the shredder, snatching the remains of the ticket from its jaws. But all it contained were the numbers she had already matched up. She would never know if it was a winner.

.⁄.

"So, how'd things go with Mrs. H?" Logan looked up from his desk as Sally walked in the next morning. She raised her eyebrows and pretended her hands shook so much she dropped her clipboard on the counter.

"That good, huh?"

"Not only that, apparently the lotto ticket she gave me was supposed to be her cousin's, and her cousin wants it back.

"Hey, if it wins, maybe her cousin will pay for a *chauffeur*…"

"That would be money well spent. If it wins..." Sally's voice trailed off as she tried to figure out whether she wanted to tell Logan what had happened to the ticket.   She remembered standing there, holding the ragged scrap of paper, wracking her brain to recall what the rest of the numbers on it had been.

"I'd lose a very lucrative revenue stream, though," he was saying "It could sink my business."

He laughed, and Sally let herself laugh with him. This was a pretty fun place to work sometimes. At least Logan had a sense of humor. She decided not to worry about the ticket. Maybe she'd buy one to replace it. Anyway, she didn't even know if it was a winner. She'd dug through the shredder, trying to find the missing pieces the night before, to no avail. It was a really good shredder.   But now a thought popped up that the cousin would know the numbers...and if it was a winner...no... she mentally shredded that whole train of thought.

"Oh, and on top of all that—" Sally was going to tell him about the cousin having a flower shop and possibly the kind of job Sally was looking for, when she realized that she probably shouldn't tell that to Logan. She stopped short as her eyes fell upon a dark figure sitting over in what they laughingly called their "reception area."

It was a dimly lit corner furnished with a couple of well-worn Danish Modern chairs and an equally shabby coffee table adorned with three or four dog-eared magazines. Unless they had been changed since she last sat down there, which she doubted, there was an ancient issue of *Car and Driver,* an outdated *Auto Trader*, a *Reader's Digest* featuring an article on our country's most dangerous roads, and a fairly recent *Seventeen* probably abandoned by a student—all in all, a pretty good representation of their customer base.

Looking over it all from the wall was a poster of some dogs supposedly driving a convertible—she wasn't sure where that came from. It seemed like a weird sequel to the paintings of dogs playing poker that she had never understood but some people enjoyed so much. A plastic plant of some unidentifiable variety completed the overall tacky scene.

But today something looked out of place. A figure garbed in what appeared to be several layers of veils and heavy black robes, topped by a pair of dark sunglasses almost befitting a blind person, sat in the corner chair reading a small leather bound volume that might be the holy book of some religion. "Who?" Sally wrote on her clipboard, and showed it to Logan.

"Let's step into my office." Logan directed her to the restroom, a tiny cubicle in the back corner of the office. They walked through the classroom in between, distinguished from the office only by a short partition, the presence of desks, and a whiteboard on the wall. Once there, he closed the door, and put the lid down. She resisted her temptation to make a joke about what it took to get a guy to put a lid down.

"Have a seat." He gave a sweeping gesture.

"So this is bad news?" She didn't need any more of that.

"Now, now, don't be so negative. I just wanted to have a conference with you about your next client."

"Client? Weren't you just explaining to me the other day that I should call them customers, because a customer is more of a short term business relationship, while a client is usually long term."

"Exactly. And I have a feeling that Sister, uh, Tsunami, just might be a *client,* you know, like Mrs. Hanama is more of a client."

"Sister Tsunami?"

"Well, yeah, it's something like that. I had a hard time understanding her accent, and I didn't want to be rude by asking a fourth time.

"Logan, that's not a name, it's a tidal disruption."

"I suggest you just call her 'Sister T.' I think she'd like that."

"I'm sure she'd like it better than being called a tidal wave."

"Anyway, she says she has a permit, but I haven't checked it, and she wants you to do an assessment of her skills so she can tell Brother Somebody how many lessons it'll take.

"Brother Somebody?"

"Something like that. He's apparently paying for it. I'm thinkin' God is behind this. Things happen for a reason, Sal, and for some reason, He decided to pay my rent this month."

"Oh Logan, don't be so mercenary."

"By the way, I would definitely spend some serious time in the parking lot on this one, Sal."

"Okay, I'll go talk to her."

Sally approached Sister T with a smile. She reached out for a handshake, but the veiled figure didn't respond. Snoring sounds emanated from the veil. "Sister?" Sally patted a bulge in the robe that she hoped was a knee.

Sister stirred. She took off her sunglasses. "You can teach me now?"

"Uh, yes, I see you've filled out the drive sheet…" Sally picked up the form from the coffee table to see if it held any clues. The ornate handwriting was nearly undecipherable. "I just need to see your permit a moment, okay?"

The sister dug in her bag, which could have held enough for overnight. She fished out what looked like a permit, but on closer examination turned out to be a state ID card.

The name started with "T," had a lot of letters that didn't seem to fall naturally into syllables, and ended in "i", so Logan hadn't been that far off. Sally decided she would probably like to be called "Sister T" But it was illegal to drive with her if she didn't have an actual permit.

"Excuse me, Sister, I need to consult with my boss."

She turned and walked over to Logan. In hushed tones she explained the situation. Logan assured her that it would be fine as long as she stayed in the parking lot because it was private property, and he was sure she wouldn't want to go beyond that anyway.

31

"Well, it appears we've got our flight clearance." She approached the veiled figure with her brightest smile and cheeriest tone. "Are you going to be able to maybe push that veil aside a bit, though, because I think for vision purposes…well, I don't mean *having* visions, of course, I just mean, you know, *seeing*." Sally giggled idiotically. Something about this woman in black made her very nervous.

"Oh no, I can do everything with these, I'm fine…" came the husky reply.

"Okay, okay, well, we'll see…" It was hard to imagine how the Sister could see to walk, much less drive. But Sally was loathe to offend her because of her religious practices. She had no idea whose wrath that might bring down on a lowly driving instructor. With the venom of her future ex already poisoning her life, she didn't need any other angry, crazed humans hell bent on destroying her.

"So have you had any experience at all, or will this be your first time behind the wheel?" Sally pushed open the door, and gestured toward the car, unable to escape the feeling that she should take the sister's arm and guide her like a blind person.

"Oh, I have been practicing some with my friend, but she doesn't have time to do very much. I want twelve lessons, then I think I should be ready for the test."

"Oh." They had arrived at the car, which was good, because Sally couldn't think of a follow-up to "Oh." She became more speechless as the drive progressed.

They lurched forward. They lurched backward. They careened around corners, and crawled down straightaways. Sally had convinced the Sister to push her veil out of the way, but it kept falling every time they lurched, which was every time they moved. The hour finally, mercifully, lurched to an end.

"I am excited. I see that I can learn. But next time I will wear something else," Sister T said, pointing to her veil.

"Oh, so you can do that?" Sally asked, stalling while she tried to figure out what to say to this woman about her driving.

"Yes, I will. So you think it is possible I can learn?"

Well, anything is possible…were the only words that popped into Sally's mind. She willed her mouth not to say them. "I think it will take a lot of lessons, and a lot of practice."

"You will write a letter to Brother recommending my lessons?"

"Um, yes, I can write a letter explaining how the lessons work, and the cost…"

"I need to learn. It will help with my opportunities. It is very difficult with just the bus."

"Oh, of course, of course." Sally nodded, wondering *what opportunities*?

Back in the office, Logan was curious. "So-o-o…your drive with the woman in black? You look a little pale."

"Did she remind you at all of the Grim Reaper, Logan? Because I just have a really bad feeling here." Sally shivered.

"Maybe…" He cocked his head a bit, considering the possibility. "So, by the way, is she Muslim? I mean, I assumed…"

"Actually not. I had her stop so I could catch my breath, and we talked a bit. She's part of some obscure cult that started on a tiny island somewhere. It's the Brothers and Sisters of the Sacred…Spirulina or something…I think she said their big holy time is when they fast and only eat dried seaweed for a month…at least that's what it sounded like. Anyway, that Rhododendron you've been meaning to prune back there—"

"Yeah, I'll get to it—"

"Don't worry about it, the Grim Reaper does landscaping."

"Oh, she wants to work out a trade for some lessons?"

"No, I mean it's done. In fact, it's not only pruned, she almost transplanted it."

"So the drive didn't go very well?"

Sally leaned against the counter. "Logan, have you considered giving me a raise? Because you know, there are other jobs out there."

"You seem pretty tense, Sal. Maybe you should take a little time off."

"Yeah, like I can afford that."

"How's the divorce going, anyhow? Any hope of a settlement on the horizon?"

"What horizon?"

"Okay, look, I know I'm your boss and everything, but how about a little dinner? Just friendly. There's a new place across the bridge that has pretty good Chinese and—"

"A good Chinese restaurant in this town?"

"Yeah, really…what do you think?"

Maybe things are looking up after all. Logan's not a bad guy, and sometimes, from a certain angle, he's really almost cute. "Yeah, I guess, what the hell, how can I say no to the boss? You might fire me from this wonderful job…"

He looked a little hurt. "Look, I mean you don't have to…"

"Oh, I'm sorry, Logan, bad joke…sure I want to go. It was really sweet of you to ask. Thanks."

He instantly brightened.

"I can't tonight, though—my lawyer gave me a stack of stuff to go through, and I really need to focus on that. How about tomorrow?

"Great." He beamed. "I'll get us a reservation."

Sally went out the door feeling a bit lighter. So what if she had to spend the evening wading through the scraps left over from a marriage to a loser? Maybe there was hope. Maybe she could still win in the lotto of love.

•⁄•

Chapter 3

*H*umming, Sally dressed for work. She was going to have a nice dinner with Logan tonight. And her lawyer had set up a meeting in a couple of weeks, saying he was working on a deal she might like. "I've got 'im on the ropes," she repeated her lawyer's words, bobbing and weaving in front of the bathroom mirror. She relished the image of her almost-ex against the ropes, both eyes swollen, a trickle of blood from the nose. And handing her a fistful of money.

She decided to email her sister the good news. Sitting down at the computer in a nook in the hallway of her tiny apartment, she reached to turn on the lamp on the shelf above. Her head slammed against a corner of the cramped cubbyhole—the same damn corner she always hit. She rubbed her head—a lump was rising. "Everything in here is so flipping *miniature*. It's like an elf apartment, or a…"

The vibration and music of her cell phone interrupted her rant. It was Henry. He'd convinced Logan to give him the number, saying his ankle was better, and he needed to schedule a drive. At first she was mildly annoyed at the intrusion, but she perked up at the words "job interview."

"Yup, I'm serious, little lady. Mildred—that's the wife—talked to Arlene, and she's pretty innarested. Call her and set it up. She wants to talk to you this week. The other girl left in a hurry, got pregnant or something, and they need somebody for Saturdays.

She took a breath. Things were really going her way. In a couple of weeks she'd have this stupid divorce settled, she'd get this job today, and she'd be in school as soon as possible. Then she could become a teacher in an actual classroom—not a moving car with students who were out to kill her—by accident, but still.

"Okay, great, Henry, thank you so much—I'll call right away."

"I was tellin' the truth when I told your boss I want to schedule a drive, too. So when can we do that?"

"Hey, listen ol' pal, I can't wait to get back in the car with you, but let's just wait until I get an appointment for this interview, okay? That way I'll know for sure when I'm free."

"Yeah, sure, I understand little lady, jus' gimme a call."

Phew. I don't want to have a drive with Henry right before the interview, and have to show up there all sweaty and nervous. She laid the phone down and began to type:

Hey, Tal—

Fantastic news on both the job hunt and the divorce. Things might be coming up roses, and I might have more than a green thumb—some actual green in my purse, if my lawyer is right. And…my love life may bloom—I have sort of a date…

I'll call you later.

Gotta go—time for a brake-stompin,' wheel grabbin' good time at the ol' drivin' school.

See ya,
Sal

.*.

The new restaurant Logan had mentioned was called "Señor Szechuan," which turned out to be, as the name suggested, half Mexican and half Chinese.

In this small farming community, she had learned not to expect too much when it came to restaurants. Oh, they were fine with home cooking, biscuits and gravy-egg-bacon-sausage- hashbrown-pancake breakfasts that would leave you feeling full well into the next day. And you could actually get good pot roast in a local café. But anything exotic—to this town Chinese food was exotic—and you were definitely taking your chances. Mexican food on the other hand was a better bet, since there was a large migrant population because of the need for farm workers.

So she had figured there was at least a fifty-fifty chance when they stepped into Señor Szechuan. The décor was…decorative. Suspended from the ceiling were large piñatas in the shape of egg rolls and fortune cookies. The waitresses wore Asian-style dresses and on their heads, yes, those were miniature sombreros.

The menu had a similar eclectic quality. It was round, one side made to look like a tortilla, and the other like a Chinese checkerboard. They offered little flat marbles for children, so they could entertain themselves while their parents ordered.

The selection on the menu was…diverse. There were a number of familiar entrees of both nationalities, but her eye was caught by the "Tastebuds without Borders" section. It featured such mouthwatering crossovers as Mandarin Mole Chicken Fajitas, Beansprout Taco Salad, and the house specialty, Szechuan Sweet and Sour Refried Rice and Beans. She perused it and sipped plum wine while she waited for Logan to return from the men's room.

A mother at the next table wiped her little girl's nose while the little twit squirmed and whined, then began screaming because her brother poked her when the mom couldn't see. Sally smiled to indicate it was all right, she didn't really mind the incessant screaming. But it was annoying. She wanted a quiet dinner. Logan must have really meant it was just a friendly dinner, because so far this place was anything but romantic.

Other people's kids didn't generally make her go all soft and gooey. She did like the teenagers she taught, and that was the age level she wanted when she got into real teaching. While teens were annoying at times, they didn't need their noses (or butts) wiped and some of them could carry on a pretty intelligent conversation. They had their problems, but she enjoyed their fresh outlook, and their forgiving attitudes. If she was late for a drive appointment, they never seemed angry—or maybe they were just hoping that meant the drive would be shorter. She knew it was excruciating for some of them to have to struggle nervously through the pain of looking stupid in front of their friends and a strange adult, but they gritted their teeth and did it. Sometimes she wondered how anybody ever survived Driver's Ed. The fragile teenaged ego craved the freedom of a license enough to put up with any torture, apparently.

She took a sip of wine, and watched the girl dump her glass of milk into her plate.

No, she never really wanted kids of her own. She was one of those people, she had to admit, who wouldn't mind having a dog, but didn't want to go through the puppy stage. And actually, she was pretty sure she'd get tired of a dog after about a month or so. She thought a Rent-A-Pet service would be nice. That way you could have fun with it for a while, then take it back when you were tired of it.

She had that kind of deal with her nieces, her sister's kids, and it was great. She could take them to the zoo, or a play or whatever, and dump them off for her sister to deal with when they were tired and cranky. She missed that. She couldn't see them so much since they'd moved.

It was probably the kid thing that had soured her marriage. Jack, her almost-ex, had wanted at least a couple. But two miscarriages had decided the issue, and she'd been secretly almost relieved. Kids were okay, she guessed, but they didn't seem worth all the trouble. It wasn't that she didn't like kids at all, but they definitely needed to be more than housebroken.

But the kid thing hadn't been the only problem in her marriage, she reflected now. *Maybe it all started when I decided to keep my maiden name, I know he wasn't happy about that, and then there was...*

"What looks good?"

She jumped as Logan appeared across the table.

"You're jumpy, Sal. Bad day of curb-surfing with the high-schoolers?" He laughed and picked up his menu.

"No, actually, it was a pretty easy one. But I guess I'm kind of anxious about what's going on with my divorce.

"So...things aren't going well?"

"They're supposed to be, according to my lawyer. It's just such a roller coaster. What if he's wrong and it's another big disappointment? He told me we're at a critical point in negotiations—he said he has them on the ropes. I'm hoping..."

"You're hoping it's almost over, and you'll soon be whisked away from this Driver's Ed hell?"

Sally laughed sheepishly. "Something like that..."

"Oh, come on, now, you don't really hate Driver's Ed as much as you pretend, do you? I mean, you're so good at it, you must like it at least a little..."

"Sure, of course, I find it satisfying, and funny…even sort of precious or something—and heartbreaking at times."

"I don't know, that sounds like passion to me, Sal." He cocked his head and spread his hands for emphasis, but in a way that she could tell he thought was sort of endearing and cute.

She thought it was mildly annoying. But she had a nagging feeling that he had a point about the passion thing. Maybe that was what annoyed her.

"My passion is for teaching. I guess I'm just frustrated that this is the closest I can get.

Especially since what's holding me back is my ex, Jack S. Morton. Or Jack Ass Moron, as I like to call him. You can call him Jack Ass, for short," she heard herself say. *Better slow down on the plum wine. And get some food in your stomach. Now.*

"Whoa…" Logan leaned back in his seat, throwing his hands up. "Maybe you need another glass of wine to calm you down a little—you are wound too tight!"

"No, no, I think what I need is dinner. That wine's going to my head really fast."

He looked a little disappointed, and her suspicious mind led her to wonder if he was actually trying to ply her with liquor and have his way with her later.

"Okay, okay, what looks good to you—on the menu, I mean."

"I'm not sure. I was hoping you'd eaten here before, and could suggest something."

They'd settled on the homemade tamales, because he said he knew the Mexican grandma who handmade them fresh daily. He was right, they were delicious. But she kept getting the feeling he was coming on to her, and that wasn't what he'd promised.

She decided then to keep things light with Logan, regardless of what he might want. Things were complicated enough. She needed a cool head.

•*•

"Just try moving your foot back and forth between the gas and the brake now, before we even shift into gear, just to get used to it," Sally said to the woman in the driver's seat. Sally glanced down at the name on the drivesheet. *Ella.* It was the day after her dinner with Logan, and she was feeling more distracted than usual.

"Which one?" Ella looked confused.

"The gas and the brake, down there." Sally pointed.

"But which one is the gas, and which one is the brake?"

"Oh-h-h." Sally felt sweat break out on the back of her neck. "See the big long one there?" She pointed.

"This one?" Ella pointed too.

"Yes, yes, that is the gas pedal. The little square one is the brake."

"Ah-h-h." Ella nodded, enlightened and amazed.

"Now try moving your foot back and forth between them. No, no, keep your heel on the floor. Good, good. That way you squeeze the pedal, not stomp it."

Ella look confused.

"It's just so you don't push too hard...or..." Sally struggled to explain 'squeeze' and 'stomp.'" She tried to demonstrate with her foot.

Ella nodded again, with an expression that silently screamed, "I have no idea what you're talking about."

They were in the big, empty parking lot of a closed-down store, near Ella's house, shortly after Sally had picked her up. Sally had chosen this lot because there was nothing to hit. Well, a couple of light poles, but they were pretty far apart.

Sally showed Ella how to shift from park to drive. "Yes, just move the gear...no, you need to press the button...oh wait, you don't have your foot on the brake...it won't move without that..."

Ella got it into gear, stomped on the pedal and the car shot forward, which seemed to scare her, because she then stomped on the brake, and they made a whiplash-inducing stop.

Sally rubbed her neck. "So now we've done some stopping and some starting. We just need to smooth it out a little bit."

"I'm driving! I'm driving!" Ella shouted happily, jumping up and down in her seat.

"Yes, isn't this exciting?" Sally tried to share her enthusiasm, but as they rolled along again her eye was caught by a sign across the street advertising yoga classes. *Yoga. I could teach yoga. I took that yoga class when my back was messed up. It was easy, and so peaceful.* She saw herself sitting in front of a class, calmly, tranquilly, demonstrating the positions in slow controlled movements…No lurching. No whiplash, no… "NO-O-O!" Sally exclaimed, as they headed straight at a light pole about ten feet ahead. She stomped her brake pedal, and they came to rest about three feet from it. *I have to focus.*

"That is stomping, or squeezing?" Ella asked, sincerely.

"Stomping, for both of us. I stomped too. We shouldn't do that anymore." Sally laughed in relief that they hadn't hit anything, and Ella joined her, probably, Sally thought, just glad that she wasn't being screamed at as she usually was, when her husband was teaching her. If there was one thing she'd learned in this job, it was that husbands should never try to teach their wives to drive. Divorce loomed just over the next hill on drives like that.

Sally's next drives were at the high school and she had to go by the office to pick up the drive sheets first. She had a half hour to get there, so she decided to call her lawyer and see how the negotiations were going. She was in the mood for some good news in the relationship department, and snuffing out her marriage once and for all would be the best news she could get about that relationship.

Now, after her drive with Ella, she was on the phone with her lawyer's office, trying not to scream.

"No, no, I'm sure he'll be ready for your meeting, Ms. Fender. He just needed a little time off. I'm sure you understand," her lawyer's secretary was saying.

"But we're supposed to meet soon, and he's supposed to be negotiating my settlement…"

"Look, Ms. Fender, he works very hard, and he's entitled to a little rest once in a while, just like you or anybody else."

"I know, I know, I'm sorry, I guess I'm just on edge, we're so close to the end, and I can't…*can't what? Can't wait? Can't control myself? Can't help acting like a complete maniac? Can't stop myself from threatening to break into his office to see if he's really there, and is just too much of a chicken to tell me it's all fallen through, and there will never be a settlement, I'll just be in Divorce Limbo for the rest of my flipping…*

"I'm sure he has the situation under control, Ms. Fender. I'll give him your message and he'll call when he returns."

"Okay, you have my number, of course. Okay. I'm just disappointed. Okay. Okay." Finally she ended the call, before she made a bigger fool of herself. No matter how many times she'd said "Okay' it hadn't convinced her. She had a bad feeling. Just when she'd thought everything was going her way, it would all turn on her. It was like that nightmare she had sometimes where she was riding with one of her students and they turned the wrong way down a one way street. She could never get them to turn around. When she grabbed the wheel it spun around uselessly. Sometimes it came off in her hands. She would scream without sound at the student to hit the brake, and he or she would just stare at her, so she'd slam hers down and the brake would go straight through the floor. Then she would wake up in a cold sweat and swear she was quitting Driver's Ed immediately, divorce or no divorce.

Then she would get up and go to work as usual. But this was no dream. Things were taking a wrong turn in her real life, she was sure. Lost in thought, she wandered into the office to pick up her drive sheets for the drives she had that afternoon at the high school.

Logan looked up from his computer. "Hey, Sal, you don't look good. Bad news from your lawyer?"

"No news, actually… But in this case I think no news is bad news. I don't know, Logan, yesterday I thought everything was coming my way, and now…"

"Well, you know the ol' Driver's Ed saying…"

"What old Driver's Ed saying?"

"Oh you know—If everything's coming your way, you must be in the wrong lane." Logan chuckled, finding himself really entertaining.

"Oh God, Logan, you've been doing this way too long. I mean, you know the old saying, 'If you're laughing at Driver's Ed jokes, you must be around the bend.' You've heard that one, right?" Sally went out the door with her drive sheets. Logan had stopped laughing and looked sort of bewildered. But in kind of a cute way, she thought.

.*.

At the high school, she and her students walked around the car, checking the tires, and looking underneath for leaks.

She tested them. "So, what if we see some green fluid down there? What would that be?"

"Uh, lime jello?" One of the girls ventured.

The other girl laughed. "No, dummy, remember in class…Coolant?"

"Oh, yeah…my bad!"

"Very good, *coolant,*" Sally encouraged.

"Oh, you know, Mrs. Fender, I saw this show where the guy killed his wife by putting coolant in her Gatorade. It was perfect you know because it's the same green and everything."

"Yes, and it has a sweet flavor. That's why his wife wouldn't have tasted it in the Gatorade," Sally added.

They looked at her, then at each other.

"I mean, that's what I've read, I don't drink it myself…" She laughed, not sure they were convinced.

"So did she just like keel over, or did it take a while or what?" the other girl asked.

"It took a while, but he kept being really nice to her, you know, so she wouldn't suspect. He kept saying how he was worried about her health, so he'd get her to work out and then say she needed Gatorade and all that."

"Eeeyooo…how sick!" The other girl curled her lip.

"I know…" agreed her friend.

I wonder if Jack would be capable... "Yes, murder is really sick…"Sally said aloud, "…to do that to his own wife…"

"No, I mean Gatorade. It is so disgusting. That taste would be enough to kill you."

Sally decided they'd talked enough. "Okay, girls, I think we've done a pretty thorough circle check. Let's hop in."

The first girl got in behind the wheel, put the key in the ignition, and started the engine.

"Whoa, cowgirl!" Sally reached over and turned the ignition off. "We have a few things to do before we actually start the engine, don't we?

The girl looked at her, mystified. "What?"

"Oh my gosh! A car jacker! Sally shouted. "Look, coming through the bushes! What can we do to save ourselves?" She affected a terrified look, appealing to both girls for help.

They both looked around, stared at her like she was insane, then the girl in the back seat had an aha moment. "Lock the doors!" She tapped the driver's shoulder.

"Oh yeah…my bad." The girl pressed the button to lock the doors.

"That's better. Now we can concentrate on getting adjusted. Which should you adjust first—the seat or the mirrors?"

"I already adjusted the mirrors. Where's the thingy for the seat?"

She pushed back with her whole body trying to get the seat to move. Her friend in back leaned forward to give her the answer. At that moment, the girl in front found the wrong lever beside the seat, and pulled it. The back of the seat flopped backward with considerable force.

"O-o-w-w-w!" The girl in the back grabbed at her face. Blood seeped out between her fingers.

"Oh God!" Sally struggled to remain calm. "Did the seat hit you in the face?"

The girl nodded vigorously, tears rolling down.

"Omigod, I am so sorry, omigod, should I call 9-1-1? Omigod," her friend babbled, tears rolling down, as she pulled her cell phone from her pocket.

"Is it your nose?" Sally turned around, leaning toward the girl in back.

The girl shook her head.

Sally dug around in the door pocket, then the glove box. She finally found a travel pack of tissues under the owner's manual. She pulled out some tissues, handed them to the girl, then got out and walked around to the back door to help her.

It was her mouth, it turned out. Her braces had cut the inside of her mouth when the seat hit. It wasn't nearly as bad as it had initially looked. Sally decided ice would be a lot of help though, to keep any swelling down. She drove them to the office, and they found some ice cubes in the fridge.

"The mom will be here in a few minutes," Logan said, getting off the phone. "She wants to take a look herself, and decide whether she needs to go to the doctor...or maybe the orthodontist."

"You doing okay, sweetie?" Sally put her hand on the girl's shoulder.

The girl nodded, holding a makeshift ice pack on her mouth, and looking considerably calmer.

"Omigod, can you ever forgive me?" her friend asked.

The girl nodded.

Sally ducked into the restroom. She shed a couple of tears of relief and release, then splashed cold water on her face. "God, usually we at least get the car moving before things go horribly wrong," she said to her face in the mirror. Then she laughed, a little maniacally she thought, but quietly so no one would hear.

•⁄•

Mrs. Hanama was next. After her experience with the girls, Sally felt a little relieved that she would be driving with an adult. Though Mrs. Hanama was a horrible driver, Sally felt sort of comfortable with her. She knew what to expect—up to a point.

"Hi, Murieta!" she said as Mrs. Hanama got in. "How was your visit with your daughter?"

"Oh, so good. We eat all the time. Here, I bring some." She handed Sally a plastic wrap covered plate of food that looked exotic and delicious.

"For me? Oh thank you, it looks yummy. I can't wait to eat." She put the plate in the back seat. *Hmm. She's giving me food, and she hasn't mentioned the ticket. It must have been a loser. Should I take a chance and ask?*

"Here, have sticky rice. You can eat that now." She handed Sally a big square of sticky rice wrapped in plastic.

Sally couldn't resist trying it. "Oh my god, that is so good. Thanks, Murieta, that was just the pick-me-up I needed. Let's get started."

Maybe it was the sugar buzz from the sticky rice, maybe it was the stress over her divorce, she couldn't really say when she thought about it later. But at that moment, her little pretend drama seemed like a good idea. She imagined that Mrs. Hanama would get a good chuckle out of it. She even thought the humor of it might be a small way to thank her student for the lovely home cooked gift.

She shot a look toward a man walking across the parking lot, vaguely in their direction. "Oh my god! Look! A carjacker! What can we do to protect ourselves?" Since she had always taught Mrs. Hanama to protect herself by locking the door, she was sure her student would reach over to lock the door, probably laughing, and say, "You trick me," or something to that effect.

She looked on uncomprehending as the woman instead grabbed her purse, got out of the car, ran to the man and began hitting him repeatedly with what Sally knew to be a heavy bag, probably painful.

The man looked bewildered, holding his arms up to defend himself and yelling things like "What the hell?" as Sally ran toward him.

"Murieta! Murieta! No! No! You're going to hurt him!"

"Oh, yes, yes, yes," said Mrs. Hanama, taking another swing.

She pulled Mrs. Hanama away from the poor guy, apologized profusely, and they got back in the car. Sally took a few deep breaths, then decided to call her lawyer to make sure there weren't any other papers she needed to bring when she met with him. That should just take a moment, and would give her time to collect herself. She reached for her cell phone, but came up empty-handed. The car had already started to roll, since Mrs. Hanama had forgotten she had to keep her foot on the brake when she released the e-brake. Sally hadn't told her to release the e-brake, but...

A feeling of horror began to creep over Sally. "Wait!" She grabbed Mrs. Hanama's arm as if that would stop the car from rolling. Then she regained her composure and hit her own brake. Too late, it turned out. She got out, looked around, then retrieved the battered remains of her phone from behind the front passenger tire. She had indeed dropped it in the rush to pull Mrs. Hanama off her pretend carjacker. *What a brilliant idea that was.*

She felt like a drowning swimmer who had dropped her lifeline. She suffered through the rest of her time with Mrs. Hanama, then went to the high school for her next drives. When she got there, she borrowed a cell phone from one of the high school kids. She stood in the parking lot listening to the phone message.

Her lawyer's office was closed for the day. But oddly, the message said they would also be closed for the next three days. It was the middle of the week, and there was no holiday. For the second time that day, horror crept over her. Something was definitely wrong. She could almost feel her brake going through the floor, the steering wheel coming off in her hands, as she walked back to the car. Then out of the corner of her eye, she caught something that made her suck in her breath so hard she hiccuped. But the sight also frightened her so much it seemed to instantly cure her of her hiccups as well. Disappearing around the corner of the building was a figure that looked for all the world like the Grim Reaper. She had a flashback of the same figure behind the wheel as they headed for a Rhododendron bush in the driving school parking lot. *Ohmigod...Sister...Whatever? That can't be a good omen. Is she lurking around my lawyer's? No, it's a small town, Sal...just a coincidence...shake it off. S*he got into the car and tried to sink into the routine.

"Okay, Brittney, enter traffic when it's safe."

"Um, could I have my phone back?"

"Oh, sure…sorry." Sally realized then that she was clutching it so hard her knuckles were white, the way her students clutched the wheel. She handed it to the girl, resolving to get a replacement after work. This was no time to be without a phone.

"Okay…now enter traffic."

"So, you're trickin' me, right, Mrs. Fender?"

"What?"

"I mean, you don't have your seatbelt on."

"Oh-h-h…good catch…Brittney…I can't fool you," Sally fastened her belt, laughing a little too much, she thought, but for once the girls didn't seem to notice.

"So, are you girls ready for your country drive?"

"Oh, cool, Mrs. Fender. I heard that's the one where we get to have the radio on."

"Right-O…we're gonna have some fun."

Fields of flowers floated by, the lovely colors alternating with the black and white of dairy herds. Sally felt better, lulled by the panorama into believing everything was really all right. She would get a new cell phone and when she dialed her lawyer's office, they would answer with a perfectly reasonable explanation. Her lawyer would be back and ready to meet with the enemy to settle up.

"What are some of the hazards we can expect in the country, Brittney?"

"Well, like, um, air pollution, I guess…"

"Yeah…" the girl in back agreed, holding her nose against the sharp manure smell.

"Okay, yeah, but I mean driving hazards, girls. Like, say, what happens if a cow…"

"Oh yeah-h-h—if a cow craps in the road that would be really slippery—you could skid! Right, Mrs. Fender?"

"I was actually going to say what if a cow were crossing the road in front of us? Or maybe a deer?"

"Oh. Well then I'd slow down and swerve around it."

"What if there's a car coming the other way, and a cliff on your right?"

"I'd—I'd—"

"What I'm trying to get at is that a lot of people get killed because of what they swerve into, so you have to be careful about swerving."

"Oh. But I wouldn't want to hit it though. That would be gross."

47

"And disgusting and cruel," came the voice from the back seat.

Sally nodded. "And it could do a lot of damage to you and your car. But what about a small animal, like, say, a rabbit or a squirrel? They can run out all of a sudden—what do you do?"

"O-o-o-h, a little bunny...well, you should slam on your brake..."

"Yeah, you don't want to squash a cute defenseless little bunny," Carly agreed.

"What if you lose control and smash into a tree because you tried to avoid the bunny?" Sally asked.

"So you should just hit the poor little bunny?" Carly asked, incredulous.

"Well, yes and no..."

"Yes and no? So I could have got it right no matter what I answered? I shouldn't have stayed up reading the chapter last night."

"It's just not that simple, like a lot of things in driving. Let's look at a situation. There was a student out on a drive with his instructor. It was his country drive, just like we're on."

"Is this, like, true?" Brittney turned to look at Sally.

Sally reached over to steady the wheel. "Eyes on the road, Brittney. Anyway, as he's driving, he looks ahead and sees a little bunny hopping across the road in front of him." She motioned with her hand to imitate a bunny hopping along. "So he turns to his instructor and says 'Well what do I do now?' and his instructor says 'You'll just have to hit it."

"Oh-h-h...poor bunny." Brittney empathized.

"Animals have rights, too, Mrs. Fender—you can't just kill them," Carly protested from the rear.

"Yeah, you could have animal rights activists picketing the driving school." Brittney shook her finger in jest at Sally.

"Keep your hands on the wheel, now...and just think about this. There was a lady driving along just a couple of years ago over in Foggy Point, and a squirrel ran right in front of her car, so she swerved."

"Good," Carly chimed in, "See, some people care about animals."

"Unfortunately, she swerved right into a power pole and killed her two-year-old daughter who was riding in the car with her."

Silence fell, as the girls absorbed the tragedy.

"So she was two years old exactly?" Brittney broke the silence. "Was it her birthday?"

"Yeah, I bet it was her birthday, and her mother went insane from grief, and ended up in a mental hospital, and…" Carly quickly turned the incident into a 'B' movie.

"Okay, okay, let's get back to the point, girls. The bunny hops across and the instructor says the student will just have to hit it, remember? And the student says 'Well, okay…' But while they were talking, of course, the bunny had hopped across the road and into the field on the other side. So the student, wanting to pass his drive, tries to do what the instructor said. He hits the gas," she made engine noises and hand motions, "and cranks the wheel to get that bunny!"

"Ohmigod! Did he actually drive into the field?" Both girls broke into giggles, and Sally steadied the wheel while Brittney recovered.

"I can't believe someone could be that dumb," Brittney said as her giggles subsided.

"Oh no, Brittney, speaking of dumb! Over there—it's Duncan! Standing in that yard. See?

"Where? Oh it is, I see him. Duncan Dix—can you believe someone would name their kid Duncan Dix? I mean that is so cruel, especially when he's such a retard anyway.

"Okay, girls, let's not use 'retard,' that's not really necessary…"

"Oh, yeah," Brittney agreed, "that was totally retarded of me. I don't usually say that—it's just from hanging out with Carly…"

"Yeah—my bad—I majorly use that word too much. But with Duncan it's hard not to. I mean, behind his back, everybody calls him Duncan Dick, anyway," Carly added.

"He's such a wannabe hick, too."

"A wannabe hick?" Sally didn't know any teen had such aspirations.

"Yeah, yeah," Carly explained. "You know, he's always wearing Carhartts, and he's got a can of chew in his back pocket, but I've never seen him actually chew, and he doesn't even live on a farm or anything, he just thinks it's cool to be a hick."

"Yeah, I know, he like moved here from California or something, and I guess he just wants to get in with the hick kids," Britney agreed. "It's kinda sad, really."

"Brittney, did you hear about when he first started in Driver's Ed and he was driving home with his parents, and—"

"And he was swerving all over, and the cops stopped them because they thought he was drunk!"

Carly and Brittney had another giggle fit, and Sally steadied the wheel.

"Fun's fun, girls, but we need to switch drivers and head back. Let's pull over up here."

Brittney immediately jerked the wheel to the right, aiming straight toward the drainage ditch, which looked to be about eight feet deep and was half filled with water. Sally grabbed the wheel.

"Let go, Brittney! Let go, I'll take over!" she said firmly but without allowing the panic she felt to enter her voice. But Brittney was frozen on the wheel. Sally pushed harder, overwhelmed her, and the car headed away from the edge and back onto the pavement. As Sally was about to breathe again, Brittney hit the gas pedal hard, and they shot toward the ditch on the other side. Sally slapped it into neutral, adjusted the wheel, and said, as calmly as possible "Brittney, get off the gas."

"Sorry—wrong pedal." Brittney slammed on the brake. They were now kitty corner across the road, and a group of motorcycles was coming their way.

"Oh, holy crap, it's probably the Hell's Angels," Sally muttered.

"No, Mrs. Fender, I'm pretty sure it's the Banditos, there's a big bunch of them that live on an old farm down the road," Carly said helpfully.

"Okay, Brittney, off the brake, I'll steer, and you just squeeze the gas— easy squeezy, okay?"

Brittney took a breath, squeezed the gas, Sally controlled the wheel, and they got back into their own lane in time to watch the motorcycle gang give them some amused stares as they roared by.

They managed to avoid any more brushes with death on the way back to the office. Sally decided she would go by her lawyer's office the next morning. She didn't have any drives until afternoon, so she would just go there and get to the bottom of this. They owed her an explanation.

.⁄.

"Oh…I'm so sorry to hear that—uh—that's terrible—I—uh…" Sally stuttered the next day as she stood in front of the secretary's desk. She had ignored the "Closed" sign hanging on her lawyer's office door and pounded on it until someone let her in. Her heart was sinking, and at the same time a voice in her head was saying that she should be feeling empathy for her lawyer. She struggled to feel the right thing.

"Yes, it's just awful." The secretary slowly turned her head back and forth, apparently for emphasis, or to show that she felt the empathy Sally was struggling to make herself feel.

Sally took a deep breath. *Sure she's empathetic, but her whole life doesn't depend on this guy being well enough to do his job. Well, actually I suppose it kinda does.*

"I just feel so bad for his family. If he remains paralyzed, it will be so hard for Cathy and the kids."

"Yes, yes, I imagine." Sally tried to force herself to wait a decent interval before asking, "Well, uh, when will we know anything about his cases? I mean, is someone taking over for him, at least temporarily?"

"We just don't know, dear, right now we don't know."

•*•*•

"So he basically took a deep dive into a shallow pool?" Logan was saying back at the office.

"Well, yeah...I guess you could put it that way, if you wanted to be totally calloused about it." It was easy to hold the high ground with Logan. "Anyway, he's lying in a hospital in Florida, paralyzed from the neck down."

"So what are you going to do, Sal? You better get a new lawyer. I mean this guy is pretty much of a stiff at this point, I'd say." Logan laughed at his own apparently unintentional pun.

"Well, I know, but when I asked his secretary about his cases, she was just worried about his wife and kids, and I didn't know what to say." Sally could feel the lump starting in her throat and the tears welling up. "Oh Logan, I just, I just don't..."

"Aw come on, Sal, don't do that..." he took her hand briefly, then gave her a tissue.

She composed herself and wiped the tears away.

"Look if you need to do that, the restroom would be better, that's all, with customers and kids coming in, you know..."

"Yeah, I know, Logan. I'm okay now. I just thought I was so close, and now I'm so far away from the end of this again. I have to figure out what to do."

"Hey, I know a lawyer. She's good, and trustworthy. I've got her number. Do you want it?

"Um, sure. Maybe a woman would be better anyway. I'm just not sure how to get out of this other thing."

"You've got a right to do whatever is best for you, Sal. It's your divorce. It's your life." He looked up at her with so much empathy, her gaze fell into his deep brown eyes, and her feelings about him wavered. *Maybe I misjudged the guy. Maybe I should give him another chance...*

Chapter 4

*H*e sounded pretty mad when he called," Logan called to her as Sally went out the door of the office the next day. She'd had a temporary brain fade and missed her appointment with Henry when she found out about her attorney's accident. She was headed out to his place now, but she wasn't excited about getting there.

It was a typical day for this time of year in the Northwest, gray and drizzly with dry intervals, even the occasional flash of sunshine today. She imagined the forecast had been "Cloudy and overcast with frequent showers and occasional sunbreaks." Just as she'd heard that Eskimos had something like thirty-seven different words for snow, she was pretty sure that Northwest forecasters had at least that many ways to describe rain. She supposed it raised ratings as people tuned in to see what creative new phrases they had coined.

As a native, she understood the finely tuned difference between "partly cloudy" and "partly sunny" as well as the meanings of "spot drizzle, marine air," and "mist turning to occasional showers becoming frequent showers later likely turning to rain" to describe various degrees of wet. As a native, she never carried an umbrella or wore a raincoat—that was for visitors and pussies. Though less discerning people said there were no seasons here, she knew there were actually two: Fall-Winter-Early Spring, and Spring-Summer-Early Fall. She silently scoffed at newcomers' inability to understand the climate.

Henry's driveway appeared around a curve. A few moments later, she turned in past the little windmill and parked. In an adjacent field, Henry was mounted on a tractor towing some kind of farming equipment. He backed up out of the field expertly maneuvering into a narrow space between a stack of crates and the side of the barn. He got down, took his work gloves off, and beat them against the leg of his Carhartt pants. He turned and walked toward the barn door, apparently unaware of her presence.

"Henry!" Sally walked toward him, flashing her most winning smile, and at the same time twisting her brow into what she hoped was a repentant wrinkle. "Henry-y-y..." She stretched his name in a way that she hoped implied the words "Ol' buddy, Ol' pal."

Henry walked toward her, but his expression didn't imply forgiveness. "It's about time you showed up. Are you gonna pay me a no-show fee like it says in the contract I'd owe you if *I* didn't show up?"

"Henry-y-y..." She had nothin'. All the way there, she'd tried to think of some sparkling banter, some smooth explanation, some sudden dire emergency that had popped up and prevented her from making it to their appointment. Tears would probably work, but that would be tacky. She had to act professional.

"That was amazing, Henry. The way you whipped that tractor and trailer right into that tight spot. There's no way I would ever be able to do something like that. I wish those people down at DOL would come out here and watch you at work—they'd be handing you a new license right now." She resisted the temptation to bat her eyelashes, not wanting to overdo it.

"Well now, my gal, I've been doing that since I was barely taller than a stalk of sprouts. Dad had me up there in his lap ridin' and helpin' steer almost before I could walk."

"A stalk of sprouts? What do you mean, like the Green Giant and the lil' Green Sprout, or what?" She tried to look as empty-headed and blond as possible. She thought she was laying it on a little thick, but the old guy seemed to be eating it up. She had to give it her best effort, because Logan had said she'd have to pay Henry a no-show fee or do a free drive, if she couldn't smooth it over with him.

"Boy you are a city girl, aren't you? You tellin' me you've never seen a stalk of Brussels sprouts?"

She shrugged. *Good. I think I've completely distracted him.*

"Just a minute," He disappeared into the barn, and returned with a thick green stalk that had small round bulbs popping out up and down it on all sides.

"That's how Brussels sprouts actually grow?" Now she was genuinely amazed. She hated Brussels sprouts and had no idea what she was going to do with this if he decided to give it to her, but still this was one of God's little miracles that she had never before seen or even thought of.

Henry looked considerably puffed up with his new found status. He was clearly smarter than she was at this moment, and all was right with the world.

"How much does one of those cost? Can I buy one?" Her sister Tally loved Brussels sprouts, and her nieces would surely be impressed with this marvel of nature.

"Open up the trunk." He walked toward the back of the car. "Consider it a tip."

With the Brussels sprouts safely ensconced in the trunk, they went out for his lesson, and the transformation was complete. When Henry felt that he had the upper hand, he drove like a different guy. He signaled, headchecked, and parked like a pro. At the end of the drive, they sat in the car talking.

"You know, Henry, I think you're ready to go take the test." He looked at her like that was a cruel joke. "No, really I do."

He let out a big sigh of relief. "Well, I gotta admit it, I'll miss you, little lady."

"Hey, you let me know how you do on the test, okay? And I'm sure we'll bump into each other at the thrift stores, right?"

"Yeah, sure, I guess..."

"Good luck, now. I'll be crossing my fingers," She opened the car door, hesitating for a moment. She felt like giving him a hug, but didn't want to embarrass him, so she reached out for a handshake instead. He took her hand, but pulled her in for a half-hug with the handshake.

As she drove away, she thought about the sprouts in the trunk and suddenly remembered she couldn't give them to her sister, because they now lived in California. She would never get used to that.

She looked up, saw a sunbreak developing, and hoped it was a sign for her life. She would check with Logan when she got back, and get the number for that lawyer.

⁂

Miles away in the little town of Clearmud, Sister T. brushed her long dark hair, then put on her heavy robe and pulled the hood over her head. She looked out the little window, and saw the sun burst through the clouds—two beams of light poking through two small openings. It reminded her of something…was it…yes, yes it was! Headlights!

Was it a vision, a message from her creator? She puzzled for a moment over the meaning of her vision. Then it hit her with a light more blinding than the sun's rays. She was going to learn to drive, after all. Though her meeting with Brother had not gone well, and she didn't think she'd ever get the money for more driving lessons, this clearly was the Lord encouraging her to try again.

She knelt for a prayer of thanks, then headed straight for Brother's office.

⁂

"Sally Fender? And you're a driving instructor? Is this one of Logan's jokes?"

Sally was sitting across from Josephine Sax, the woman Logan had recommended to replace Sally's now paralyzed attorney. Sally was still trying to get her money back, but Josephine had agreed to take her case without a retainer as a favor to Logan. Josephine, Sally discovered, was a friend of Logan's mother. She was certainly old enough to be, Sally mused as she studied the roadmap of wrinkles that marked Josephine's face. She watched the frail-looking woman pick up her cane and hobble to the door, almost losing her balance as she closed it. Seventy? Eighty? Sally tried to guess the woman's age, wondering herself if this was one of Logan's jokes.

"Yes, that's correct," Sally said, meaning to answer the first question, then realizing too late that it sounded like she was agreeing that her name was a joke.

"I knew Logan was up to something,"

"No, I meant my name is Sally Fender, but it isn't a joke. It's my real name, I never changed my name when I got married, and then I got into Driver's Ed by chance…"

"Oh." Josephine sounded faintly disappointed. "Well. Let's get started then. You're getting a divorce? Did you bring everything I asked you to?"

Sally handed over the files she'd brought, hoping it was everything needed to free her at last.

As Josephine picked up the files she knocked over a picture on her desk. She picked it up and handed it to Sally. It was an elderly black man kneeling by a black and grey dog of some sort. Sally was not a dog person and had no idea what make or model this particular animal might be.

"Cute dog," she said. "And who's the guy?"

"That's my husband, the old reprobate. He died fifteen years ago today." She gave a wistful look, then replaced the photo.

Sally shifted in her seat. Maybe this wasn't a good day to start things out with her new lawyer. Maybe she should shop around a bit.

Josephine peered from beneath her wrinkled brow. "So your boy is quite the S.O.B. from what Logan said?"

Sally began to like her. "Yes, he's dragged this out, and made things as difficult as possible."

"And what do you want out of this?"

"I want to go to college and become a teacher."

"I was a teacher once, but I just couldn't stand those obnoxious little twerps and their sniveling parents. So I became a professor instead."

"Oh."

"You'll find your place, dear. Just don't get your hopes too set on any one thing. Now, what do you have to have?"

"What do I need?"

"What do you have to have out of this?"

"Well, I mean, as much as I can get, so I can afford college and everything…"

"Here's what we're going to do—" The phone rang, and Josephine answered. The conversation seemed to be with another lawyer. "Yes, yes, Bob, it's in the statute, I don't recall chapter and verse off the top of my head, but it's there. Let me think about it, I'll get back to you later today." She hung up looking annoyed. "Dammit." She tapped her index finger on her forehead. It's in there somewhere. I'm getting so forgetful."

"I'm sure you'll remember whatever it is…" Sally hoped she would remember whatever it was. She wanted a lawyer who could remember things, especially about the law.

"It's just so damn frustrating, sometimes. You know, I used to have a mind like a steel trap." Josephine shook her head slowly back and forth. "Now it's more like an electric tie rack. I know the thought is in there, but I just have to wait for it to come around in its own clicking time."

Sally laughed. "You're not alone in that. Sometimes the stress just gets to me and my brain freezes up. "I completely forgot my appointment with this old guy—senior citizen—the other day, and he was p—mad" *Don't let your hair down too much Sal, you don't know her yet.*

"So the old guy got pissed at you, eh?" Josephine chuckled. "Yeah, they'll do that." She picked up the files, looking directly at Sally for a moment. Sally felt she was being sized up.

"I'll look these over, and you decide what you have to have. Then we'll meet again, say, next week?"

"Sure, okay, that sounds good." Sally got up to leave. She reached out for a handshake, and watched as the woman she was leaving all of her important papers with reached out too, knocking a coffee mug over onto them.

"Whoops! It's okay dear, just a few drops. It was almost empty. I'll see you next time, and we'll get this show on the road."

Sally walked away wondering what kind of show this would be, and if this road was going to take her in the right direction, or just be another wrong turn in the fog.

.*.

"Hmm. That big lotto winner still hasn't turned the ticket in." Logan was staring at his computer screen as he chewed on a sub sandwich when Sally came in. "You're not holding out on us, are you Sal?" Logan chuckled.

Sally's heart fluttered. She decided to change the subject. "No, I'm still trying to win some money in my divorce." She laughed weakly.

"So, you saw Josephine, right? How'd it go?"

"Okay, I guess. She's…well, I was going to ask you, I mean, she's up in years…she's not, um, you know…?" Sally tried for a tactful way to put it.

"Senile? No, no…she's sharp as a tack, especially for her age. Josephine has saved our family's butts again and again over the years. You should have met her husband, Vernon. He was quite a guy."

"So she said."

"Oh, she told you about him?"

"Well not really, we mostly talked about what I should get from the divorce."

"Get all you can, Sal, you deserve it."

"She seemed to think I should just get whatever I absolutely have to have." Sally felt she should have more than that, by far. She wanted everything back that she'd put into it, she wanted money for damages, she wanted money for pain and suffering, she thought a short jail term for him might be appropriate, she thought…

"Sal?" Logan said, "did you like her?"

"Who? Oh—Josephine? Yes, actually, I did kind of like her. I just wonder if I should shop around a little. I mean, it was really nice of you to recommend her, but…"

"So you have other money? Or did you get the retainer back from Diver Man?"

Sally had forgotten momentarily about that little problem. No money. No shopping.

"Logan, you shouldn't call him that. This is really a tragedy for him and his family."

"Okay, take the high ground, but he's still got your money, doesn't he?"

"Yeah, that he does. I'll probably need a lawyer to get it back. So I guess Josephine is my gal."

"You'll never regret it, Sal. I mean it."

"What, are you getting a commission or something?"

Logan looked genuinely hurt.

"Okay, okay. I'm sure you just have my best interests at heart." She patted him on the shoulder.

"I do, and I wish you'd believe it." He actually sounded sincere.

•⁄•

Mrs. Hanama had an idea. She was pretty sure it was a good one. Sally, she had decided, was just as nice as she seemed. Her divorce was probably all her husband's fault. So it was time to go forward. Her son, Robert, was a nice boy, but even as his mother she had to admit he was lazy. He needed to get out of the house and get his life started. Sally was such a nice person, and though she was a bit older, Mrs. Hanama thought that might be a good thing. She could teach him. He needed guidance.

But how to get them together? He already knew how to drive. She had thought and thought. But today she felt she'd hit on something. Maybe…yes, *maybe*…

•/•

Sally sat in the car finishing up paperwork from her last drive as she waited. She watched Mrs. Hanama for any sign of "Where's-my-cousin's-big-winning-lotto-ticket" look on her face. Surely she would have already said something, but…

Moments later Mrs. Hanama got into the driver's seat. She looked over at Sally.

"You think my son ride along sometimes? He could help me practice if he watching how you teach me."

"How old is your son, Murieta? You never mentioned him before."

"Oh, he twenty-seven. He working at the bowling alley. And at the miniature golf they have outside in summer."

"Well, yes, of course, he's certainly old enough to help you. Bring him along to observe next time, if he can."

"I doing that."

"Good, good. Now let's head up the highway today, and work on curves some more. You're getting better, but we still have a ways to go on those." Sally was trying to relax. She'd been meditating before work today, as Tally had suggested. Tally was a great one for all that kind of stuff, had even made her own drum out of a piece of elk hide. She'd proudly explained the whole process as she showed it to Sally. She belonged to a women's group and some old Indian guy had done a workshop for them.

Tally had moved to California, because her husband had gotten a job there. It had worked out well, because she could keep a closer eye on their mother, who lived in a retirement community or whatever they were called. It was one of those deals where they had different levels of care for different degrees of decrepitude, sort of like the seven circles of old age hell. Sally didn't want to get old that way. She didn't want to get old at all. If she ever got into a state like some of the people she'd seen there, parked in a wheel chair in a dead end hallway smelling like pee and mumbling through puckered dentureless lips, she had told Tally to just put a gun to her head and pull the trigger. Tally had looked shocked—and assured Sally that she would change her mind as the years went by—but she had agreed, at least in theory, to do this one favor for her big sister.

Or "big little sister," as Tally referred to her. Tally had always been the grounded, mature one, wise beyond her years. An "old soul," as she said her women's group referred to her.

Tally and Sally. Sally could not fathom why her parents had named them that way. It might have made sense if they were twins or something.

Her mother's favorite aunt's name had been Sarah, so that's what she'd named her first born girl. That made sense, Sally guessed. Her father liked nicknames, and he called her Sally. Then the second girl came along, and all her mother had were boys' names. She hadn't had an ultrasound, but had gone to a psychic, who informed her the child she was carrying would be a boy. Then Tally was born, and their mother named her after her own grandmother on the spur of the moment. That would have made sense too, but their mother always talked about how much she hated that grandmother. Still it would have been okay: Sarah and Talia; that sounded fine. But her mother never thought ahead to nicknames. Her mother never thought ahead period.

Her father again chose a nickname, and that was when the feces hit the fan. He immediately gravitated to "Tally". He thought it was cute. Sally and Tally. Sally adored her daddy, so she gritted her teeth, and bore it, but she hated it. It emphasized her immaturity, brought her down to her little sister's level, made them sound like twins. She loved Tally, but hated their names.

Mrs. Hanama was talking about "Robert." Robert this and Robert that. Sally was just about to ask who this Robert was, when she remembered Mrs. Hanama had been talking about her son earlier, and Sally was pretty sure his name was Robert. She knew Mrs. Hanama would be offended if she had forgotten his name already, so she just listened along, hoping a clue would drop that would confirm who Robert was.

"...and buy his own bowling alley and golf course. That one is a smart one, he could do it. He just needs pushing."

"Oh, well, you know a lot of people are like that when they're that age." Sally tried to remember how old Robert was. She was pretty sure that's who they were talking about, from the bowling alley comment.

"I talk him into coming along next time. He can get up a little earlier. He don't having to work till afternoon. Maybe you can go bowling together some night?" Mrs Hanama smiled the hopeful smile of a mother trying to marry off her first born son.

Sally swallowed her latte wrong, then looked up from her coughing to see that the car was aimed so that her side would almost certainly sideswipe a power pole that was unusually close to the edge of the road. She was holding the latte in her right hand, always mindful of keeping her steering wheel hand free, especially with Mrs. Hanama. She jogged the wheel and they were back on a safe course.

"You be good bowler," Mrs Hanama observed. "Good eye, quick reflexes—I bet you bowl a strike every time."

Sally just coughed.

•/•

Later, Sally sat in her big comfy chair after work. It was the most luxurious item in her cramped apartment, and took up half of the living room. It was worth it. Her back always ached at the end of her shift, after sitting for hours, tense every moment, waiting for disaster to strike, huddled on the broken down seats of Logan's beater cars.

Besides her sore back, she had noticed she was developing another occupational hazard: spreading butt. So instead of the Haagen-Daaz she craved, she was eating a low-carb ice cream bar, and dipping it in a tub of non-dairy sugar free low fat whipped topping. Before each bite she scooped the fake-chocolate covered bar through the white fluff, coming up with a sizable dollop which she then licked off, pretending it tasted like whipped cream instead of air.

Air and what? Thicker air? Yes—air combined with really thick air that had been somehow dyed white. Or painted white. Because when she thought about it, it tasted just like what she imagined white paint would taste like. Still, it looked luscious before she actually put it in her mouth, so she kept on, hoping as she followed the trajectory of each fluffy bite toward her mouth that this one would be more delicious than the last—meaning it would be delicious at all.

Her phone jingled its happy little tune, one that she was sick of, but she couldn't decide what to change it to. She'd put this one on to cheer herself up and convince her that when the phone rang, it would be good news. Instead it just annoyed her with its perkiness, and when the news was bad as usual, it was more of a letdown. Maybe a funeral dirge would be better, then whatever came after would seem good. She pulled the phone from her pocket.

"Hello? The male voice that responded had a tone of dejection. "Henry?"

"Yeah, little lady, it's me, and uh, things didn't go like I planned at the DMV."

"DOL, Henry, we don't have a DMV in this state. But what happened? You were doing so well."

"Uh, yeah, DOL. Well, my ankle isn't quite right, I guess after all, an'...uh, it had some kinda spasm an' I hit the gas when I shouldnta, an' I knocked over one a them drive test signs an' they don't want me back for a while."

"Oh, Henry, I'm so sorry. Did you see the doctor?"

"Yeah, he says he thinks it didn't heal right an' the bone might be putting pressure on a nerve or something, so they have to do an MRI, an' see what's going on. So the upshot is, I'll be needin' some more lessons before I go back to the DM—DOL, if they let me back in, that is."

"Oh, Henry, I'm sure they'll let you try again. I'm sure they've seen worse than that." *Hell, I've seen worse than that.* "And I'll be happy to give you some more lessons. You know that. I'm sure it won't take much anyway. You're basically a good driver, you just had a few bad habits, and once that ankle heals right, there'll be no more problems, right?"

"Well, I sure hope so, little lady. This really threw me for a loop. I kinda feel like I been drug through a knothole backwards."

"You just call me when you're ready for a lesson, okay?"

There seemed to be a hesitation at the other end.

"So, is there anything else, Henry?"

"Well, uh, I got kinda one of these bad news-good news deals you hear about, ya know."

"And…"

"Yeh, I know ya really wanted that job doin' the flowers, but I guess Arlene's niece kinda stepped to the front of the line on that."

Sally's heart fell.

"But there's good news, too, like I said."

"What's the good news?"

"Well, ya know there's these doings for the tulip festival comin' up...and Arlene's been asked to do kind of a demonstration deal for that."

"Oh. Um, that's great. I'm sure she's happy about that." *So...what? Are you just rubbing in that I didn't get the job in the flower shop to make yourself feel better about your ankle?*

"No, see, she's not exactly that happy because she gets really nervous in front of people, and her niece is even worse, so she won't help. I guess it runs in the family...anyways she was wondering, since you're a teacher and all, if maybe you could give her a hand. She'd pay you and everything, she doesn't expect you to just do it for free."

"Henry, that sounds great. I'm really excited. Arlene and I should get together and plan what we're going to do."

"Now the pay's not much, you know. Don't get too excited."

"No, no, not at all, I'll enjoy it no matter what the pay."

"Okay, well, I'll have her give you a call."

"Perfect." Maybe she'd keep that perky little tune after all. Maybe it was bringing some good news her way. A flower show. She could maybe make some connections there. She'd be doing a demonstration—that had to give her some real credibility. Maybe there was a market for that. Maybe flower people needed people like her to help them with demonstrations. There were lots of odd little job niches that you didn't know about until you stumbled on them. Maybe this was one. She saw her exciting new life, traveling from city to city, flower show to flower show, demo to demo, wowing people with her skills at teaching people to arrange flowers. She might become a flower arranging guru, writing books about the Zen of tulips, and doing book tours in between her flower tours and...

The phone sang out in her hand. It was Tally. Sally began telling her little sister all about her new career, the words spilling out so fast they seemed to fall one on top of the other. After a couple of minutes, Tally stopped the torrent with a question.

"So you've talked to a publisher? You actually have a book deal?"

"Well, not exactly, I mean I was just sort of projecting the possibilities. I didn't mean..."

"Oh. I'm sure it'll work out great for you though, Sal."

Sally could hear the puzzlement in her little sister's voice. At that moment Sally knew why she was such a good driving instructor.

"You know how good I am at pretending, Tal. I sit in that car all day pretending I'm not nervous at all, pretending people are doing a great job of driving, pretending they'll all really get licenses. And all the while pretending I'll get my divorce any day now, and get a settlement big enough to go to college and be a real teacher, and live a happy life, and it's all just one of my daydreams." The last couple of sentences she boo-hooed her way through, and Tally jumped into her usual role of consoler and encourager.

"No, no, Sally, it'll be fine, you'll be great, things'll work out, they always do."

"Yeah, for the worst they do..." Sally was in full sob now, and not in any mood to be consoled.

"Okay, okay, Sal, they'll be terrible. That's what you want to hear so you can really enjoy your cry."

Sally stopped in mid-sob. This wasn't the pattern. This wasn't Tally's role. *What is going on?*

"Look, Sally, I actually called about a problem I'm having down here, if you have time for that. Mom is acting a little weird, and I need to talk to you about it."

"Weirder than usual?"

"Yeah, definitely. You know that old sword of Dad's?"

"The antique one from the Spanish-American War..." Sally knew all about that sword, from the foundry where it was made to which great-great uncle wielded it in the war.

"I don't know—I guess that's what it's from—anyway she was sort of *wielding* it at the nurse's aide and the girl really freaked out, so I had to do something. I mean, I know mom wasn't actually going to do anything, she was just annoyed with the girl, and honestly she is pretty annoying, but they were going to kick her out. They said I had to get rid of the sword before mom hurt someone."

"Well, of course, I'll take it. I've been waiting to get it from her. Dad said I could have it when he died, and then mom swiped it." Just holding it made her feel closer to her dad. Sally felt tears starting and bit her lip. *No tears. I'm the big sister, and I'm going to act like it.*

"Okay, well, it's too late for that—I gave the sword to Uncle Bob, so it won't be a problem anymore, but..."

Sally heard the scream for a couple of seconds before she realized it was emanating from her own throat.

"Sal—What? What's wrong—oh my god! Is someone attacking you? I'll call 9-1-1!"

"No! The sword!" Sally managed to choke out.

"They're attacking with a sword?"

"No! How could you give away Dad's sword? Tally, how could you possibly?"

"Uncle Bob was happy to get it. He thinks it's a collector's item. He's going to try to get on *Antiques Road Show* with it. I had to get it away from Mom, she was going to get kicked out of her place."

Sally's body took over. She could not control the tremors that shook every part of her.

"I didn't know you wanted it, and I mean he's Dad's brother, they were close..."

"I told you before that I wanted it."

"Maybe you did. I forgot. Dealing with Mom takes a lot out of me, you know? Look, there's lots of other stuff. There are boxes and boxes at Mom's place, and the way she's going downhill, it won't be that long before we're going through it. She's not that old, but maybe Dad's death was harder on her than we thought, who knows? Anyway, you can have first choice of Dad's stuff, okay?"

Sally was too upset to speak.

"Hey, I have to go now, mom's doctor is on the other line, and I've been waiting for his call. I'll call you later and fill you in, okay?"

Sally croaked something that must have sounded like "Bye," because the call ended, and she was left shaking, her insides churning. She remembered...smelled a whiff of her father's aftershave as he swung the sword, heard the whoosh and felt the air riffling her nine-year-old hair. "It's all yours, Sal Gal," he said. When I'm gone, it's all yours 'cause you're the oldest."

She remembered forcing down the disappointment when her mother had kept the coveted object after her Dad died. "I'm just not ready to part with it. You understand, honey," Her mother had explained. Sally hadn't understood, and thought her mother was just torturing her, but tried to be mature about it, and waited as patiently as she could.

❖

"Dammit!" Logan was clearly not happy, and Sally was rethinking her plan to ask for time off so she could go to California to get the sword, and clarify with her big little sister how she felt about what had happened.

"These stupid damn people! I am so tired of instructors who have go to the bathroom every hour! There aren't enough bathrooms in the world for these people!" He turned toward Sally. "How often do you go to the bathroom, Sal? Okay, I know that sounds stupid, but I do have a reason."

"Well, I usually wait till the end of my two hour drive, and take a couple of minutes then, but I can wait like, four hours, if needed. I have a pretty strong bladder, actually. But I do need to go right now, if that's okay." She pointed toward the office bathroom.

"Sure, sure, of course, but I want to talk to you when you're done. I have a proposal for you," They exchanged looks. "I mean a very professional one, and I think you're going to like it, just to clarify," he said.

Sally sat ruminating in the postage-stamp-sized space that was the driving school restroom. Definitely not ADA approved. A wheel chair would get wedged into that doorway, permanently. But then Logan didn't have an instruction car with hand controls, either. It was too small a company to afford that kind of expense. She wondered if Logan would ever get into the big leagues with the schools that had cars like that, or even had new cars, and paid their employees benefits, or never mind benefits and new cars—had just one piece of new furniture in their office. More important, what was the proposal he was talking about, and why did it have so much to do with her bladder?

Oh jeez. There's no toilet paper. She felt around in her pockets, where she could usually count on finding an old wad of tissue left over from an allergy attack. Nothing. *I've got some in my purse.* She dug around and came up with an empty purse-size tissue pack. *Damn.*

The paper towel dispenser would have been the obvious choice—in a normal restroom. But this was Logan's restroom. A few months before, the dispenser had broken, and Logan had a deal with the landlord that he would fix things himself in exchange for cheaper rent, but it was even cheaper not to fix things at all, and he hadn't fixed this yet. Usually there was a pile of paper towels on the little shelf above the sink—but not today. She gazed around hopefully. At least it was reasonably clean. No grey patina of grease covering everything like her mechanic's bathroom.

Dave's girlfriend Gwelda did the cleaning on weekends, or it would probably look a lot worse. Her eyes fell upon the wastebasket just beyond the sink. It was full. She glanced at the door.

Oh god, the door is locked, isn't it? It would be bad enough to have someone see her with her pants down. But being seen rummaging through the bathroom garbage with her pants down? That would be sort of like being seen with your pants down twice, wouldn't it? She reached over and checked the door. This, she thought, was one advantage to such a minuscule bathroom.

Clenching her nostrils at the thought of what she was doing, she tried not to hear the annoying scraping sound as she pulled the metal rust-spotted waste can across the concrete floor. God. Even for a wastebasket it was disgusting. *I have to make Logan get a new one.*

She peered in, nostrils clenched tighter. Good. No used tampons visible... a crumpled note of some kind... probably written by one of the kids, piqued her curiosity. She couldn't resist the temptation to read it. That could be pretty funny. Definitely worth a look. She lifted it up to reveal a very promising apparently unused fast food napkin just lying there waiting, not so much as a wrinkle or a ketchup splotch. Pristine. She uncrumpled the note, then sat blotting with the napkin in her left hand while she read the note in her right.

"Look I just want to tell you," it said in very scrawly teenaged boy-type handwriting. But the next few words were completely scribbled out and she couldn't make out any of them. The next line was "I'd really like it if you could…" and more scribbles, then "and I think I could pay for that, at least." Then more scribbles. She decided it would be fun to show it to Logan. They could fill in the blanks for a few laughs. Setting it on the edge of the sink, she pulled up her slacks, silently having a moment of gratitude for fast food, and the napkins that came with it. Then she washed her hands very thoroughly. Glancing around one last time for a hidden stash of paper towels, she blew on her hands briefly before giving up and wiping them dry on her slacks. After a quick check in the mirror, she headed out to the office to share her find with Logan and see what his little mystery involving her bladder was.

Logan was on his cell phone, jotting something on a notepad. She looked down at the pad as she waited. *God, it's amazing how grown men can have such scrawly, boyish hand—oh shit.* She looked down at the note, then at Logan's writing again, then discreetly crumpled the note back up and stuck it in her pocket.

"Logan, the paper towels and toilet paper are out again."

"Yeah, okay, Gwelda'll be in later, I'll have her take care of it. She's gonna be in the office more now anyway."

"Why? I thought she drove you crazy."

"Gwelda drives everybody crazy, including Dave."

"Then why is she his girlfriend?"

"I don't know, you'd have to ask Dave. Anyway, I promised him I'd give her a job filing and answering phones and stuff."

They both cast a glance at the general disarray—the snowdrift of paper that was his desk, the haphazard piles of files stacked on the floor behind it.

"Well...even though Gwelda drives me nuts too, you really could use some help with the filing."

"Yeah...and it's an easy enough job...she's done okay with the cleaning...so I thought I'd give her a shot. And you don't have to worry, you won't be in the office too much anyhow if you accept the offer I have for you."

"Does it have something to do with my bladder?"

Logan laughed. "Yeah, kinda...I need somebody up in Cement Falls, and there ain't a lotta bathrooms, so a strong bladder is a must."

"No bathrooms? Don't they at least have an outhouse?"

"The high school locks up a half hour after school, and you're driving till eight."

"There aren't any restaurants or anything?"

"Well, there's a gas station, but it just has a porta potty, and I heard it's pretty disgusting."

"But it's good enough for me?"

"No, that's not what I mean...but all the other instructors I've sent up there apparently have to go to the bathroom every hour, and it's a real problem. You know, I thought maybe if you only have to use the porta potty once in a while..."

She looked at Logan as he spoke. He was shifting uncomfortably in his seat. This couldn't be what he'd had in mind when he'd thought about having his own business, being the boss. She couldn't help feeling sorry for him.

"And I'll pay you for an extra hour for the long commute..."

She was about to say "sure, Logan," when he continued:

"And I pay an extra dollar an hour up there, but how about another dollar, since you're helping me out?"

She wondered if she should speak, or if it would be more profitable to wait a second. "Okay," she said, "I guess I could do that," *Maybe I can afford to fly to California and get that sword back, after this.* "But I need you to do something too, Logan."

"Sure, Sal, what do you need?"

"*You* need to do something about Dave! The kids have told me he takes them to garage sales on their drives. And yesterday, a girl told me he took her on the freeway on her first drive, so he could get free coffee at the rest area. Isn't that illegal even? I know he's your brother and everything, but he's really weird."

"Look, Sal, you haven't been doing this for very long, so I'll give you a clue—everybody in this business is really weird."

Sally had suspected this. But she had been clinging to the notion that in their hearts they were all saints, deputized by St. Christopher himself to selflessly save young lives through education.

"Think about it, Sal. How many adults want to spend all day every day hanging out with a bunch of fifteen-year-olds? Not just hanging out—we put them behind the wheel knowing full well they have no clue how to drive, then tell them to hit the gas, and hope we come back without crashing. And the clincher: *We enjoy it.* Anybody who stays in this business does it because they love it. Sure we complain about the scary ones, sure we go get bombed after a really nerve-shattering day, but we come back and we do it again because we're addicted."

Addiction. Love is one thing. But addiction? Sally rolled her eyes.

Logan went on: "It's the adrenaline, Sal. We're all closet adrenaline junkies. We could get it by skydiving or bungee jumping, but we want more than that. We want to feel that we are the kind of people who risk our lives to save the lives of others, and teach them how to save themselves in the process. We're adrenaline junkies who are also wannabe saints."

Sally gasped. She felt she had just been stripped naked in public. *Oh my god. He knows me.*

Logan looked into her eyes. And the look said he-knew-she-knew-that-he-knew. Something had happened between them.

•/•

70

Chapter 5

Early the next morning, Sally yawned as she cruised up the two-lane highway toward Cement Falls. She felt tiny against the deep green hillsides. Thick fingers of mist crept down the slopes, looking like a calendar photo more than real life. Though she wasn't a morning person, the crisp air of early morning had exhilarated her, and the beauty all around raised her spirits. All this, and extra money, too!

She glanced down at the seat. Yes, on her clipboard she had the kids' drive sheets, and some extra blank ones just in case the wrong kids showed up. She was ready. *Mistake. Don't ever think you're ready for this job. You're just asking for it.*

A little while later, she pulled into the Cement Falls School parking lot. The school was made up of two buildings, one for grades 1-8, and the other 9-12, with a gravel lot between them.

Beneath the overhang at the front door of the high school stood two teenage girls. One wearing a baseball cap with her brown ponytail sticking out the back, and a tall blonde dressed in jeans, a hoodie, and flip-flops, who walked over to the car as Sally pulled up. Sally rolled down the window, and the blonde leaned down to talk.

Sally grabbed her clipboard. "I'm Sally—Sally Fender, your instructor for today. Are you, uh, Samantha...or Kayla?"

"Kayla...but I don't have my permit. Is that a problem?"

"I can't let you drive, then. You should know that from class, Kayla."

Kayla looked around. "Who would know?"

71

Sally could see the point. Emptiness in all directions. And it wasn't like there were a lot of cops around here, or that the cops would probably ever stop them anyway. Unless they got into an accident, which with her luck would definitely happen if she let the girl drive without a permit.

"I would know." Sally looked directly into Kayla's eyes. "And Samantha would know."

"Oh, Samantha doesn't care, and she won't tell anyone, will you, Sam?"

Samantha giggled, shrugged and shook her head all at once.

Kayla pressed on. "But I know exactly where it is, Mrs. Fender, could Sam drive there so I can get it?"

"How far are we talking about?"

"Oh...like five minutes...right, Sam?"

Sam nodded, shrugged and giggled all at once. "Don't worry, Mrs. Fender, I'm a really good driver." She reached down for the adjustment bar as she slid into the driver's seat. "I drive all the time with my dad, and like he showed me how to pass this semi on the right, down the shoulder and—"

Sally stifled a gasp. "Okay, you can take us to get Kayla's permit, but no passing on the right, Sam, or I'm taking the wheel."

They drove along a winding road much more than the promised five minutes, but Sally didn't really care. She let herself relax and enjoy the scenery. They turned a couple of times, ending up in a small logging town: old houses, pickup trucks, plaid shirts and high water jeans. There was an old-fashioned cafe, and her heart leapt with the belief that it would have a bathroom, but it was closed down, an "Out of business, thanks to the government" sign on the door. No traffic lights, a few logging trucks—one with a faded bumper sticker that said "I love spotted owl, it tastes just like chicken."

They pulled up beside an old Buick. Kayla jumped out. "This'll just take a second, Mrs. Fender." A few minutes later, after what appeared to be a thorough search of the Buick, she was walking back toward the Driver's Ed car. "Damn," her lips were saying.

She frowned as she plopped into the back seat.

"Shit! I mean, shoot. I know I had it. I was drivin' with mom yesterday, and I—" She covered her mouth, eyes wide with a sudden realization. "Oh, god. Can we go one more place? It's only a couple blocks, I promise."

With Sally's nod, Kayla leaned forward and whispered in Sam's ear. Sam shrugged, giggled and covered her mouth, then put the car in gear and pulled out. They cruised past a vacant lot full of tall grass and rusty old cars, turned on a dirt road, and parked in front of an old house.

Kayla opened the door and got out, then turned and leaned back in. "Can Sam go, too, Mrs. Fender? I might need help."

"Uh...well, maybe if..."

"Thanks—C'mon, Sam, get your hands ready, girl!"

Both girls jumped out of the car, giggling. Sally watched as the girls tried the front door, which was apparently locked. As they disappeared around the back of the house, Sally had misgivings. *Maybe I should have checked this out, knocked on the door, found out who lived here and if the girls had any business...oh god.*

She leaned over to look. The girls were at the side of the house now, and she could just see Sam giving Kayla a boost up to a window. Kayla was almost twice Sam's size, so they teetered precariously, but managed to stay upright while Kayla pounded, then tugged on the window.

I should go stop them. As Sally reached out to open the door, Sam gave Kayla a push and she wriggled in through the now open window. Sally pulled her hand back from the door, deciding it might be better to just wait in the car. Sam disappeared around the back of the house. Sally guessed Kayla had probably opened the back door.

She checked her watch, then turned on the radio. A song called "I Just Want to Sex You Up" came on. She looked toward the house, shuddered, and switched the radio off. A few minutes later, the girls came out the front door, and got into car, out of breath and giggling.

Kayla climbed into the back seat. "I can't believe Brett was still sleeping!"

Sam laughed, and turned toward her. "Ohmigod...I can't believe you actually stepped on his..." She glanced toward Sally, then covered her mouth and giggled some more.

"I know, you'd think that would have woke him up, wouldn't you?"

Sally turned toward Kayla. "By the way, did you find your permit?"

Kayla pulled a bent paper card from her pocket, beaming.

"So, this is just a paper temporary. It's still good but you have to make sure you get the permanent one before it expires, okay?" Sally handed it back. "Now, is there any place else you girls want to stop, or do you have a few minutes for a driving lesson now?"

"Well, I'm starving...do you think maybe we could swing by Country Fries Drive-In for some burgers?" This was apparently hilarious, because both girls dissolved into terminal giggles, and it was another five minutes before Sam could resume her drive.

•⁂•

Three days later, Saturday morning, Sally pulled into the Cement Falls High parking lot again. Kayla and Sam walked over to the car, Kayla waving her permit and smiling.

Confused, Sally checked her schedule. "Wait a minute, girls." I show three boys driving. I'm supposed to do a three-hour drive with them. Are you early?

"Maybe a few minutes." Kayla nudged her partner. "Pretty sure we're not three hours early. Are we, Sam?"

Sam giggled and shrugged.

Sally saw movement behind the girls, and around the corner of the building came three boys, randomly nudging and punching each other as they made their way to the car.

"I think you might be."

The girls turned to see what Sally was looking at.

"OMG, Sam—DeShawn and Jason and Chance. They're not supposed to drive, are they?"

Sam giggled. "I told you…"

From the way Kayla was looking at Jason, though, Sally had a feeling this wasn't necessarily a mistake. Kayla moved toward the boys as though planning to go along.

"Maybe one of us could ride along and observe, since we're here, anyway…ya think, Mrs. Fender?

"Don't think so, Kayla. It's the boys' turn. I'll see you two later."

•⁂•

Sally looked over at the young man in the driver's seat, his hair in dreadlocks, his large brown hand slung over the top of the wheel, arm outstretched as he reclined in the seat.

74

"Okay, DeShawn, let's get your seat and mirrors adjusted before we go. How about if you get that seat pulled up a bit, and you get both hands on the wheel, down at 9 and 3, you know, like a clock? That's the best hand position, so that your arms are away from the air bag."

"Oh yeah, Mr. Weber said it could break your arms if it pops out. So why would you want an air bag if it's gonna break your arms, I mean how is that safe?"

Sally explained to him that it was safe and could save his life in a crash, there was just a slim chance of injury if his arms happened to be in the way because of the force with which the airbag deploys. She heard herself saying all this as she had many times with many students. But she felt she was listening to herself from a distance because her real attention was on the far more interesting conversation going on in the back seat.

"Yeah, that's the car I'm getting, that white one." Jason was pointing to a picture on his phone.

"Looks like a bar of soap with the corners knocked off." Chance smirked.

"Dude, that's harsh. So, what kind of car you gettin'?" Jason demanded of Chance.

"Oh, I'm not right now. I got into a little trouble."

"You're not grounded, are you? Are you still going to the dance Friday?"

"Totally grounded. Can't even come to school anymore."

"How come?"

"Got expelled, 'cuz I set fire to this girl."

While DeShawn fiddled with the mirrors, Sally turned around enough to see the incredulous look on Jason's face. He then laughed the nervous disbelieving laugh that teenagers do when they don't know what else to do. When he stopped, Chance adjusted his cap, then explained, "Well, it was on accident."

"You set fire to someone…accidentally?"

"Justine—I think her last name's Samson or something."

"You accidentally set fire to Justine? Dude, I went out with her once last year."

"Okay, so, I was just lighting my lighter, and I lit it too close to her shirt, and it caught fire…I mean, it not like big flames or anything…but you know, the way a rug or blanket does, that's what it did. The teacher said she must have been wearing a lot of hairspray, and that's why."

Sally wondered if she really did want to teach in a public school.

Jason was still laughing, and repeating, "Dude, I can't believe you actually set fire to her…"

"Well at least I put her out," Chance defended himself.

"You threw water on her?"

"No, I just beat on her and stuff."

"You set her on fire and then beat on her?"

"I was putting her out. Anyway, the teacher said she must have been wearing a lot of hairspray. So, that's why I got suspended." He brightened. "I'm looking at it as an opportunity. It's a chance to do better next year."

The rest of the drive went along pretty uneventfully, with no one getting set on fire. When they got back to the school, Kayla and Sam were there waiting.

Kayla got into the driver's seat, Sam was in the back.

As they cruised along the main street of town, Sally suggested that Kayla do some "commentary driving."

When Kayla stared at her blankly, she explained, "You know, where you talk to me about the signs, and the possible dangers that you see? You learned this in class. Remember, you tell me what you see as a driver who is scanning the traffic scene?"

"Okay. Oh, Sam, look at that old lady, isn't she cute?" Kayla was clearly not getting the idea. "I think old people are just so cute."

"I know, especially like when it's an old man and an old lady, and they're like walking down the street holding hands…"

Sally looked at the old woman in question, and tried to fathom the cuteness these girls were seeing. "Okay, that's not the kind of commentary I had in—NO, WAIT! PULL OVER!"

"Right here, Mrs. Fender?"

"Right here. I'll be back in minute."

They stopped in front of a house with several cars parked around it. She opened the door, and jumped out of the car. As she glanced back, the two girls looked at each other and giggled, shrugging at the antics of their crazy driving teacher. She didn't care. This was perfectly reasonable. *I'm not Dave. I'm not going to use any of their drive time to do this. We'll drive extra time on the end. Anyway, I've never gone to a garage sale on a drive before.* But she had to do this. If she gave such a great gift to her nieces, Tally would be reminded of what a wonderful sister and aunt she was. She might soften and see to it that Sally got her father's sword. Maybe not, but at least it would make Tally look bad.

The girls piled out of the car to join Sally, who was in the middle of the garage sale examining a very large oblong box. The picture on the lid showed a trampoline. A middle-aged man came up to her.

"It's still in real good shape, and all the pieces're there. Your kids'll love it. Those both your girls?"

"What? Oh, no those aren't my kids...they're Driver's Ed students."

"Oh...I wondered. When you pulled up, I saw the sign, and fer a minute, I thought you were deliverin' a pizza."

"Does anyplace around here actually deliver?" She lifted the lid on the trampoline box and peered inside.

"Uh...no...That's why I wondered."

"Oh. Well, listen, I'm in kind of a hurry. How worn is this?" The trampoline was rolled up tight, and while she wanted to pull it out, she was pretty sure it would take way too long to unroll and reroll it.

"We've had it for a couple years, but the kids never wore shoes on it, and it's just been boxed up in the garage lately."

"How much do you want for it?"

"A hunderd dollars."

"How about seventy-five?"

"I'll have to talk to the wife. She said a hunderd." He went into the house, and returned a few moments later, shaking his head.

"She said a hunderd."

"Tell her I'll give her ninety." If it wasn't in good shape, she could bring it back. She knew where he lived, after all.

He went back in, then returned smiling. "She says okay, but you gotta haul it outta here right away before the kids get back from Saturday school. They didn't know she was selling it."

"Sure, no problem. I'll write you a check. Boy, my nieces are gonna be so thrilled. They've wanted a trampoline forever." She handed Trampoline Guy a check, then turned and went toward the car. She looked at the trunk of the small compact car, then at the trampoline box, then at the trunk.

"Oh...jeez...the car. Uh, look, I was thinking I had my hatchback...I don't usually go to garage sales at work...Uh—well, let's try...maybe it'll fit."

They all tried to wrestle the unwieldy box first into the trunk, then the back seat…then the trunk again. It was clear that the best bet was the trunk, but even that was pretty iffy. They set it on the ground leaning up against the car while Sally took the jumper cables, fire extinguisher, first aid kit, and absolutely everything else she could find in the trunk, and put it on the floor of the back seat. She knew this went against everything they taught in Driver's Ed, since you were never supposed to have heavy objects loose in the car with you, because they could slam into you in a crash and kill you. It seemed at that moment that she'd been brainwashed in Driver's Ed training. She was slowly turning into some kind of Driver's Ed zombie. She had even gotten into the habit of seatbelting her groceries in, which she felt really stupid about when people saw her do it, but it was like her brain was growing this whole extra "driver's ed lobe" that she could no longer control.

"I guess you'll just have to let it stick out of the trunk," Trampoline Guy offered.

"Driving all the way down the highway to Mount Overlook like that could be a problem."

"Yeah, I see that…But the wife was real plain, though…I got some rope in the garage. Probly if ya tie it down it'll be okay."

"But if anybody sees me…" Her driver's ed lobe was active again.

Kayla had a suggestion. "If we can just get it in good enough to go a few blocks, we could leave it in Brett's garage till you can pick it up."

"You think that would be okay?"

"Sure, Brett won't care."

"But what about his parents? I mean, he does have parents doesn't he?" Sally was beginning to wonder.

"He just lives with his uncle."

Sam shrugged. "Yeah, and his uncle is unemployed, so he's usually out hunting or fishing. Or else he's drunk."

Kayla nodded. "Believe me, he won't care."

"Well, if you think so…I guess I don't have a better idea…Okay, let's do this, women."

They wrestled the box into the trunk and with it teetering precariously, drove off laughing.

•/•

When Sally got back to the office, Logan didn't look good. "What's up, Logan? You look pretty unhappy."

"Sal, it could all be over. Everything I've worked for. This whack job of a woman could bring it all crashing down around me."

"What whack job?"

"You know that mom of the kid Dave supposedly called a 'horrible driver'?"

"Yeah, so she's still around?"

"Not only is she around, she's been talking to DOL. The head of the program called me." He ran his fingers through his thick hair, then took a sip of coffee.

"So what can they really do about it? I mean, he may have called her kid a horrible driver. How bad is that? He denies it anyway, it's his word against the kid's."

"Yeah, if only that were all."

"What else?"

"She's been talking to other parents who say Dave has taken their kids to garage sales, using their drive time. And he's had them stop at the casino so he could go in and play the slot machines."

"Oh…God." Sally broke out in a sweat thinking of her trampoline adventure. But she really hadn't used any of this kids' time. She made a mental note never to do anything like that again.

"Anyway, they're investigating."

"So, what could happen?"

"Worst case, I could lose my school license, and be shut down."

"But do you think that would really happen? I mean wouldn't Dave just lose his instructor license instead? He's the one who's doing it, and you can't exactly watch him every minute when he's out in the car…"

"Yeah, I know, but I'm ultimately responsible for what my employees do out there."

Now Sally felt awful about the trampoline. On top of that, she had realized on the way home that she had no idea how she was going to get it to her nieces in California. She probably wouldn't really go down to get the sword. She had some vague idea about going down to see them for Christmas if things worked out, but nothing was certain, and how would she take this huge box on the plane? And now it was clear how big a risk she had taken for something so silly.

She also felt really bad for Logan. She couldn't help being impressed by the way he was taking responsibility. Of course, she had tried to warn him about his brother…

The look on her face must have spoken volumes.

"Yeah, I know, you tried to tell me."

"Oh, Logan, I don't feel like saying 'I told you so' at all."

"Well, you did, and I guess I should have listened. But he's my brother, and it's hard for me to believe some of these things."

"Have you actually talked to Dave to get his side of the story?"

"No, I just got off the phone with DOL. I'm going to talk to Dave, and then to Josephine. If any lawyer can fix this, it's her. By the way, how's she doing for you on your divorce?"

"I don't know yet, really. She's talking to his lawyer, and then we're supposed to meet."

"She's good, Sal, you'll see."

"If she is, then she can probably help you out of this, Logan. And hey, maybe things aren't as bad as they seem. Maybe Dave can explain. You know the kids can make things sound worse than they are sometimes."

"Yeah, maybe you're right. Maybe…" Logan paused and seemed lost in thought. Then he looked up at her. "Thanks, Sal."

"Sure, Logan. If there's one thing I've been trying to learn lately, it's that things aren't usually as bad as they seem."

"Yeah… hey look, I was planning to go to this conference that's coming up, and I probably won't be able to now, but they have these things periodically, and you can learn some good stuff at them, and I was wondering if maybe sometime you would want to…you know they're usually at nice hotels and we could—I mean—I don't mean—oh shit…"

"You think I should go to one of these conferences, and it would involve staying overnight?" Maybe Logan wasn't such a sleaze after all. Maybe he was just really clumsy at things like this.

"Yeah, and I could probably pay, I mean the company could pay, at least some of the expenses, if you were interested. Because actually, you have to do some continuing education to keep up your license, you know."

"I know, and I was wondering about how I was going to do that, and this sounds like it might be a good idea." Was this what the crumpled up note was all about? But why was Logan stumbling over something perfectly legitimate professionally…unless he had more in mind to do in the hotel room than study driving instruction...or maybe he really was just clumsy...it was hard to tell.

"Really? You think so?"

"Sure, I'll think about it."

"Great, Sal, great."

"How're things going up in Cement Falls, by the way?"

"Great."

"No problems, you know, fitting it all in, or..."

Sally's heart skipped. "Fitting it all in?"

"Yeah, I know it can be hard to find places to do some of the maneuvers up there like parallel parking and stuff, so are you able to fit in all the necessary requirements, or do you need some help with the routes, or..."

"Oh..." Sally laughed. A little too much. "No, no, no..." And said "no" too many times. "No, I'm doing fine, as far as fitting it all in goes."

"Great. That's one of the marks of the kind of instructor I need, Sal. You have to be flexible, be able to get the lay of the land, and find the routes wherever you are. Which reminds me, I need you over in Foggy Point to do Dave's drives. I've got to meet with him about this other thing, so if you could sub for him over there that would really help."

"Sure Logan, happy to."

•*•

Arlene, Henry's friend, called later, wanting to get together about the flower program Sally was to help with. Since her drives in Foggy Point the next day weren't until the afternoon, she stopped at Arlene's flower shop on the way.

With Sally's ideas, they were able to outline a really good presentation. She could see that Arlene was impressed. Arlene even suggested that if this went well, she might need someone to help her with a whole series of presentations for the annual Tulip Festival. Maybe Sally was on her way to bigger things after all. Maybe she would be able to cut back on driving instruction soon, and coast to her divorce doing something much more relaxing. Pursuing the possibility of a flower shop job seemed all the more important, considering her conversation with Logan. She didn't want to be unfeeling about his troubles, but she did have to take care of herself

It would be good practice for the teaching profession as well. Doing this plan had been like doing a lesson plan, and now she visualized herself in front of a class, and felt she could really do it. She would talk to Logan about maybe subbing in some of his classes. He had told her before that she would need to get more experience before she tried classroom, but now she felt ready. She was also going to talk to Arlene about setting up regular classes in flower arranging. She had lots of ideas, and Arlene seemed open to listening.

Yeah, wait till she told Tally. They hadn't talked since their conversation about the sword. *I want everything to be okay between us, but I'm not groveling. I was not wrong this time. And she was so doubtful about this whole flower thing, but now I'm really making things happen.* Driving toward the ferry terminal, Sally felt a rush of adrenaline as she contemplated the new direction her life was taking. But this was good adrenaline, not like the kind she so often had with, say, Mrs. Hanama.

She took a few deep breaths and tried to settle down to the coming task. She would be picking up a group of kids who were coming over from the islands. Logan held classes over there, but the kids had to do at least part of their drives in a more urban area to get any serious driving experience. There wasn't even a traffic light over there.

It poured rain while she sat in the car at the ferry terminal. She wanted to go in and get a latte and something to eat. The ferry from the islands was coming in, but hadn't docked yet, so there should be time, she thought. She listened, and at the sound of the rain slowing down, jumped out and dashed for the terminal, holding her clipboard over her head, paper side down. Around her tourists watched, amused—she was pretty sure they were tourists, since they all had umbrellas and raincoats.

Once inside, she finger-combed her hair, then studied the espresso stand's wall menu. Ah…hazelnut, her favorite flavor, was today's special. She dug into her purse and counted up her cash. *Enough for a latte or food, but not both. Well, maybe biscotti…Wait a minute, that banana is still in the glove box from yesterday…that'll be a good healthy lunch.* She now sat at one of the small round tables sipping her latte through a straw, and watching for the kids to get off.

Three teenagers caught her attention as they came through the wide door into the small terminal. Their fidgety bewilderment set them apart. She walked over to them, holding her clipboard in front of her, hoping that would help identify her. She glanced around. No parents in sight.

"Dillon, Brianna, and Skyler?" She looked at them expectantly, sincerely hoping they were the ones. She didn't want to be accused of accosting someone's children in some inappropriate way.

"Are you the driving instructor?" One of the girls asked. Both girls had short dark hair that looked bottle black, with identical lip piercings. In fact, they looked pretty identical except slightly different clothes. They had to be twins. She checked the last names on the drive sheets. They were the same, which pretty much clinched it.

"Where's Dave—Mr. Nash?" asked the boy.

"He had a schedule conflict, so I'm your instructor today. My name's Sally." She reached out to shake hands. She felt that learning to drive was a big step into the adult world, and often did things like shaking hands to treat her students like adults, but it just confused this guy. He put his hand up for a high five, looking lost about why her hand was down so low. They made a connection somewhere in between, and managed something that might be loosely described as a fist bump.

"And you are?"

"Uh, Dillon."

"Okay, Dillon, I need to see your permit, and everybody else get yours out, too." She checked his, then one of the girls handed hers to Sally. "Okay, Skyler, looks good, and how about you, uh, Brianna?" As she glanced down at the drive sheet to make sure she got the other girl's name right, something seemed amiss. She glanced back up in time to catch the tail end of what looked like a permit pass. Skyler appeared to have passed hers to Brianna.

"Okay, let's see, Brianna."

Brianna now thrust the permit toward Sally, with her thumb conspicuously over the name, apparently hoping Sally would just check the date quickly enough not to notice this was the same permit Skyler had handed her.

Sally took the permit from her hand, and the two girls exchanged a look.

"Yeah, so this is not your permit, Brianna."

"Oh, um," She put her hand over her mouth and giggled. "I must have grabbed the wrong one, uh…"

"Okay, so show me the right one."

The girls looked at each other again. Brianna went through the motions of digging into her purse.

"So, is it actually gonna cost $40 if she doesn't have her permit?" Skyler asked.

"Yes, I'm afraid so. I can't legally drive with you unless you have your permit."

Skyler began helping her sister dig through her bag, which would take a while to fathom the depths of, from the size of it. "Oh, score, here it is, Mrs. Fender. It's a little bent, I think it went through the wash, but…see, Brianna, your paper one is in here."

Brianna looked at Skyler, then seemed to pick up her cue. Oh, yeah, I forgot I had that…"

"If you have already gotten your hard copy, the temporary paper one is no good, girls."

"Uh, no her hard copy hasn't come in the mail yet. It was weird—mine came, but hers didn't," Skyler explained.

"Wait a minute, I can't read the name…"

"Uh, yeah, like she said it went through the wash… but the date says it's still good, and that's her in the picture…" Skyler had all the answers.

"Yeah, but the number's wrong, Skyler."

Brianna's face fell. She knew she was busted.

"What do you mean? How do you know what her number is? It's her number, not yours…" Skyler wasn't giving up.

"Because the number is part of your name, as well as a bunch of numbers. This is your number, Skyler. See the last name, then the first letter of the first name. If this were Brianna's that would be a 'B.' Pull yours out, and it will match this, because this is your paper copy, isn't it?"

Skyler blushed, then her tough exterior softened, and she looked close to tears.

Dillon looked away, and shifted his weight from one foot to the other.

Brianna put her hand on her sister's shoulder. "It's okay, Sky."

Sally was puzzled. *Why is Sky so upset? It's really Brianna's problem. Just twins being close?*

Brianna explained. "Sky borrowed my purse last night when she went to the dance, and then left it at her boyfriend's house. My permit was tucked in the inside pocket, and we didn't have time to go get it this morning before the ferry, because she got up late. So mom will be really mad at her if it costs $40."

"Can I just drive for two hours, and then Brianna can drive for two hours next time?" Sky's voice was shaky, and her chin quivered ever so slightly.

Shit. "No, I'm sorry, I really can't do that, girls. It's illegal for you to drive for more than an hour."

"Dave would do it," Skyler muttered.

"Yeah, Mrs. Fender, Dave never even checked our permits last time," Dillon joined in for the first time.

Damn Dave. "I don't know what happened last time, but legally I can't drive with you unless you have your valid permit with you. I'd be risking my instructor's license. I'm sorry." Three sets of teenaged eyes glared at her. Her stomach growled. She looked at her watch. She had drives later, but if this drive ended early, she would have time to run home and have an actual lunch instead of just a banana. "But what I can do is just drive with the two of you who have permits, and I'll write off the fee, since it wasn't exactly Brianna's fault." It would mean an hour she wasn't getting paid for today, but she still remembered how hard it was to be a teenager.

Skyler blotted her eyes on her sleeves and brightened. Brianna breathed a sigh of relief. Sally felt better too. You never knew what went on in these kids' homes. She figured sometimes they deserved a break more than she knew.

"So, who wants to drive first?"

Skyler volunteered, and they drove toward Chagrin Cove, since this was supposed to be their "country drive," and that direction put them on some high speed, winding roads.

"All right, Sky, what does that sign mean?" Sally pointed to a warning sign with a silhouette of a car above two wavy lines.

"Uh...Uh..." Skyler was stumped.

"Is it 'wavy road'?" Dillon volunteered.

"Actually, I was looking for 'slippery when wet.' And since it's pouring rain, we need to be extra cautious."

"Okay, so should I slow down?"

"Yes. And turn up the wipers. They need to go faster to keep the windshield clear."

Skyler looked down toward the wheel, and started fumbling with the turn signal lever. "Where are the wipers?"

The car had started to veer dangerously toward the centerline. Sally steadied the wheel. "The lever on the right," she said. "Remember, you're supposed to find all those things when you do predrive? You know, the Cockpit Drill?"

"Oh, yeah. I forgot to do that." Sky turned the wipers up, and Sally let go of the wheel.

"How about if you hydroplane, what should you do?" Sally asked.

"If you hydroplane? You mean like boats?"

Dillon again volunteered. "Me and my dad go down and watch the hydros all the time. He takes a cooler full of beer and food and stuff. These friends of ours have a nice cabin cruiser, and they always tie up to the boom at the Seafair race. So we meet them at the Marina, and—"

"I meant the kind of hydroplaning you learned about in class. You know, where you drive through puddles, and the car begins floating on a thin layer of water, and you lose control. So you let off the accelerator…"

"Oh." They all said in unison.

"Did we have that in class?" Skyler asked the other two.

"Yeah, maybe, I'm not sure…" Brianna said.

"I'm pretty sure you did," Sally said with finality. As they drove along, she looked out the window, enjoying the scenery. Lush green forest came right up to the edges of the narrow winding road. On the right, the landscape dropped steeply down. On the left it rose just as steeply. Not a house in sight. She was formulating a question about what to do if the wheel drops off the edge of the road when Dillon leaned forward and spoke.

"Mrs. Fender, I have to go to the bathroom really bad."

"Uh…could it wait a little bit, Dylan? I don't see a restroom."

"I don't think so. I mean, I drank two mochas on the ferry and I didn't have any breakfast, and it kinda went right through, I think."

"You were on the ferry for how long?"

"Um, about a couple of hours."

"You couldn't have gone then?"

"I hate going on the ferry. It's too weird."

Both girls nodded in agreement.

"Oh, yeah," Skyler said. "I never go on the ferry. Bree, remember that time that lady came up to me in the bathroom, and said she knew Mom…"

Bree did remember. "Oh yeah, she was definitely a creeper."

"Y'know, we had never seen her before, and I think she just like wanted to touch me, y'know because she put her hand on my arm and called me 'honey,' and me and Bree ran out of there so fast…"

"Well, no, I didn't mean weird that way." Dillon leaned forward again, squirming a little in his seat. "I meant it's just weird to go to the bathroom when you're floating on water, I mean, what if you pee or even poop on a fish? It just doesn't seem good for the environment. And what if somebody catches that fish and eats it right after you like went, on its head or something? I can't wait any longer Mrs. Fender. All this talking about water made it way worse."

Sally watched for a place that was a little less steep, and with a wide spot to pull over. On a sharp curve ahead there was a viewpoint. "Pull over up there, Sky."

"Up where?"

"There! You see the viewpoint?" They were getting close, and had not slowed down at all yet.

"Viewpoint?"

"The gravel spot!" Sally started braking and reached for the wheel. She couldn't afford to miss this, and take a chance on Dillon not being able to hold it any longer.

Skyler looked down at the floor. "There's something wrong with my brakes," she said, panic in her voice. Next the engine revved.

"No, it's me—I'm braking for you," Sally explained. "Take your foot off the gas." She said this calmly, reaching over to the gearshift and tapping it into neutral for good measure. "Steer us into the viewpoint, Sky."

"Oh, I thought I was on the wrong pedal."

"I know. It's all okay now, I've got the brake, just turn a little more. There we go."

They came to a not-too-jerky stop, and Sky remembered to set the parking brake. "Good job, Sky. Okay, Dillon. Go for it."

Dillon headed for the bushes. Sally decided this was a good time for a snack. She opened the glove box and got the banana out.

"Ooh, that makes me hungry," Bree said from the back.

"Yeah, Mrs. Fender, do you think we could stop for something to eat?" Skyler was eyeing the food. "We have money, and I know Dillon does too."

"Yeah, maybe when we get there we can grab a snack. We'll want to get out and stretch a little anyway." Feeling sets of hungry eyes upon her, Sally stuck the banana back in the glove box. It was time to go anyway. Dillon had just reappeared from the bushes.

They made the rest of the trip uneventfully. As they came into the outskirts of Chagrin Cove, Sally began looking around for a fast food place with edible food. Then she remembered she didn't have any money. Or not very much.

"Okay, turn right into this driveway...into the parking lot, yeah," she directed Sky. "Now, remember the reference point: turn the wheel when the first line looks like it's under your side mirror...no, not yet....Sally reached over and held the wheel, briefly preventing her from turning. There, now...and straighten it up as the car is almost straight...yes, yes, perfect! Open the door and see how you did." Sally opened her own door and looked down. "I've got about a foot between us and the line—is that what you have?"

"Um, yeah, about a foot, I guess."

"And it looks like we're straight, too." Sally pointed down at the line. "Awesome!"

Sky blushed at the compliment.

Sally set about combing every pocket of her purse, hoping she'd missed something earlier. She came up with a quarter and a wad of paper that she was pleased to find was a dollar bill. Together with what she had left over from the latte, she could get something off the dollar menu, and a drink.

"We can pay for yours, Mrs. Fender," Sky offered. "Mom gave us way more money than we need, huh, Bree?" She turned to her sister.

Bree nodded. "Yeah, it's totally okay, Mrs. Fender."

Sally was pretty sure it wasn't okay to have the kids buy her lunch. "Oh no, no, I'm fine, but that was really nice of you girls to offer. The big question we have to answer now is: who feels ready to take us through the drive-thru window? Sky? Dillon? We're going to switch drivers either before or after we eat, depending on who is up to the drive-thru task..."

Before she could finish, Dillon was already unbuckling his seatbelt. "My dad made me drive through one the other day, and it was a piece of cake...I'll do it, Mrs. Fender."

Sky breathed a noticeable sigh of relief before unbelting and getting out to switch places with Dillon.

"Looks like there must have been a midget driving." Dillon adjusted the seat to accommodate his long legs.

Laughing, Sky reached up and punched him lightly on the shoulder. "I'm not a midget—*retard*!"

"Okay, you guys, that's inappropriate—no 'R' word and no making fun of people's height."

"Yeah, Andre the Giant, watch your mouth!" Bree piped up, and all three dissolved into laughter.

A few minutes later, Dillon was aiming for the drive thru. "My dad has an SUV, and it's totally different than this. I can't tell how close I am—am I doing okay, Sky?"

"Dude, you're asking me?"

"You're sitting on the same side of the car as me, so you can see how close we are."

"Well, you're on the same side of the car as me, and you're way taller than little midget me, so you should be able to tell way better than me!"

"I know, right!" Bree joined in, fist-bumping her twin.

"Okay, okay, I'm sorry about the midget thing, will you just help me a little, I've only done this once."

Sally jumped in then. "You're not in any danger of hitting anything, in fact you really need to get closer. Turn the wheel about a quarter turn to the left."

"Are you sure? I feel like I'm gonna hit it." He turned just slightly left, then suddenly swung the wheel to the right. They arrived at the window at least three and a half feet away from it. Dillon rolled down the car window, beaming. He then looked out, and finally realized how far away they were.

Sally checked her mirror only to see a car pulling in directly behind them. "We can't back up. Can you reach, Dillon?"

"Pretty sure those Andre arms are long enough," Sky said to her sister.

Dillon glanced back. "Yeah, I heard that—hey maybe I can just toss a midget over to get the foo—"

"That's all, you guys—"

"We're just kidding, Mrs. Fender, we always do this," Bree offered.

A smirking young man took their order, and Dillon dropped about half the money as he leaned out to pay. He opened the door to pick it up and left it open to get out and take the food and drinks. The kids in the car behind them honked, pointed, and laughed. All in all, it wasn't pretty, but they got their food and survived lunch with only a minor ketchup mishap when Sky squeezed the packet too hard and it squirted onto the seat. After some bleach wipes and a healthy dollop of antibacterial soap, they were pretty sure it wouldn't stain.

As they were leaving the parking lot, they bumped hard over the curb. It was a fairly high one, and Sally heard metal scrape. She had Dillon stop while she took a quick look under the car before they pulled out. Thankfully things looked okay.

They were rolling smoothly along on their way back toward Foggy Point when Sally felt her phone vibrate. *Maybe it's Tally—I'd better check.* It was Josephine. Sally tried to answer, thinking she would just tell Josephine she'd call back after the kids were safely deposited at the ferry. She'd be between drives, and have plenty of time to talk then. But Josephine's voice kept cutting out and the call dropped before the conversation even got started.

"Whee!" Dillon was saying.

Sally snapped to attention. "What?"

"We just went through a traffic light. I've never driven through one before."

"Oh." Sally then remembered they didn't have a traffic light where they lived. "Well, uh, it was green wasn't it?"

"Yeah, I think so..."

"Was it green, girls?" She turned around to see that Bree was apparently asleep, and Sky was playing a phone game. "Hey you two! You're supposed to be observing! Sky, wake Bree up, and turn that phone off."

"Okay, okay..." Scowling, Sky nudged her sister.

"Look, Sky, driving is just like real life, you know—you have to be present to win."

"Oh, yeah...well isn't Dillon supposed to be present then? He's driving...and anyway, you're the instructor, shouldn't you—"

"Never mind, we have to focus. There's a red blinking light coming up.

"So, what does the blinking red mean, Dillon?"

"Stop?"

"Good. And that was a nice, smooth stop, too." They sat in silence for several seconds. "So, it's all clear isn't it?"

"Um," he turned his head both ways, laboriously checking for traffic. "Yeah."

"So what are we waiting for?"

"Uh, I guess I was waiting for the light to stop blinking."

The guy behind them leaned on the horn. "Let's go," Sally said.

As soon as they were safely across the intersection Dillon said, "It means stop and then go when safe, right?"

"Or four way stop, right," Sally confirmed.

"I just spaced out for a minute because I saw a cop back there."

"Oh, I—a cop?"

"And he just turned his lights on."

She saw it in her mirror as Dillon spoke.

"What do I do? What do I do, Mrs. Fender?"

In back, the girls were jumping up and down in their seats. "Let's outrun 'em! Maybe they'll even pit us!   We might be on the news!"

"QUIET, GIRLS! Okay Dillon, just relax and we'll look for a safe place to pull over." Sally's heart was pounding so hard she was afraid the kids would hear it. *Was that light we went through red? Is it because we were holding up traffic at that blinking red? What can they really do? Oh god, Logan's investigation! This could make everything worse! Could I lose my license, too?* She tried to remember back to her training. She thought the ticket went to the student, because that was the driver, but....

"Ohgodohgod, Mrs. Fender what do I do?" Dillon hyperventilated the words.

Sally's phone began to vibrate. *I'm not checking. That's probably how we got into this.* "Okay, see that wide spot?"

"No. Where?"

"Right there, it's coming up, you're going to miss it!" She reached over to grab the wheel but he fought against her attempt to turn it. The wide spot wasn't very long, she'd have to yank hard on the wheel or better yet knock his hands away and steer them in herself at this point but that would panic him even more, and who knew how he would react? It was probably too late to get into it anyway, so she decided it would be safer to let it pass. "Okay, Dillon, when I see another spot, I'm going to help you pull over, so you just try to relax and let me help, all right?"

"Am I gonna get a ticket, Mrs. Fender?"

"Just relax, and don't worry about that now. Take it one step at a time." Fortunately, after the next curve, she saw a "Slow Vehicle Turnout" sign. "So, do you see that sign, Dillon?"

"Please don't test me on signs right now, Mrs. Fender, I'm really nervous, and all that pop I drank went right through me so I need to go to the bathroom again."

"No, no...I'm not testing you, there's a long turnout coming up, and we're going to pull in there, okay?"

"Is there a bathroom?"

"I don't think so. Can you hold it till the next gas station?"

"I'm not sure."

"Well, maybe there are some bushes."

With Sally steadying the wheel, they were able to pull over smoothly and come to a stop without any further problems. The problems began after they stopped. Dylan swung the door open, undid his seatbelt, and before Sally could stop him, jumped out and ran.

"Isn't he supposed to sit with both hands on the wheel till the cop gets here, Mrs. Fender?" Sky asked.

"Yeah, that's what the book said," Bree added.

"Dillon, wait!" Sally leaned and shouted out the still-open door. But then she saw what his hurry was. About twenty yards away, next to a pile of construction materials, was a porta potty. He was already halfway there. She turned to see what the cop was doing. He seemed to be messing with something on the seat next to him. Now he looked up. She had a feeling she needed to act, and act fast. She jumped out of the car at the same time he did, but he was reaching for his gun. She held up both hands.

"WAIT! He's just going to the bathroom!" she yelled. "WE'RE DRIVER'S ED!"

"I know!" the officer yelled back, gun now drawn. "But I have to follow procedure! I need to see his permit, before he goes anywhere!"

Dillon had heard, and he now turned to face them. He saw the gun, and his hands shot up in the air, a terrified look on his face.

"It's okay, son, but I'm alone, so I have to be careful." The officer approached them as he spoke. "Just use one hand, reach into your pocket, and get your permit. Then walk over and lay it on the hood of the car. I'm going to walk toward you as you do it." The officer walked over, and checked the permit Dillon had carefully laid on the hood. Dillon stood watching, both hands up.

"All right, son, go take care of business," the officer said, a smile in his voice. Dillon took off running. "Look, ma'am—you're the instructor, right?"

"Yes, I'm Sally Fender, officer."

"Well, look, I might not have handled things just that way, but there's been a series of break-ins in the area, and a young suspect is on the loose. So I had to be extra cautious, you understand?"

"Oh sure, sure officer, you're just doing your job."

"Anyway, the reason I wanted to stop you in the first place—"

Now it was time to take her medicine. In her mind she began to construct what she hoped would sound like a reasonable explanation for why they had run a light, when she had a brake on her side to prevent such dangerous mistakes by the student.

"...and they said you went over the curb as you left the lot," he was saying, "and that's apparently when it fell off. So when I came through the drive thru just after that, I offered to try to try to catch up with you, or drop it by the office on my way through town. I was going that way anyway, so it was no problem. They gave me a description of the car and a partial plate, but honestly the way you were driving made it pretty easy to spot you. Here, let me go get your sign." He turned and walked toward his car.

So the sign fell off, and he was just trying to catch up with us to deliver it? I checked underneath, but I knew I should have walked around back. But really, that's all he stopped us for? The simple reality of it began to sink in. She felt the knot of tension in her chest release. She began to breathe normally again.

She saw the cop lean into his car and pick something up off the front seat. *The sign. That's what he was messing with. And maybe that's why that guy leaned on his horn. He didn't know we were Driver's Ed. Or maybe he was just an asshole. Who knows? Who cares? I'm off the hook...*

When they finally arrived back at the ferry terminal in Foggy Point, everyone was worn out. The kids waved a limp goodbye, and headed for the ferry. Between the stop for lunch and getting stopped by the cop, Sally's slack time was almost eaten up. She used the restroom, then checked her voicemail while she waited for the next set of students.

Josephine had left a message that Sally should call and set up an appointment. Josephine had had a long talk with the almost-ex's lawyer, and was expecting a settlement proposal shortly. Tally's message just said they might have an opportunity coming up that she wanted to talk to Sally about.

Sally sat in the car pondering who to call first. She decided on Josephine, since she could call Tally that night after she got home.

•/•

Sister T finished her prayer with a few thoughts for her driving instructor. Brother had given his consent for Sister T to take more lessons, and she wanted to make sure her instructor was safe. She had been such a nice young woman, and Sister couldn't wait to resume learning from her.

But there were preparations to make first. The funding had to be approved by Brother's supervisor. And she had to get some different clothes. Brother had decided it would all be okay, because he needed someone to drive the youth van to their activities every week. He had been doing it, but apparently his nerves were not well suited to driving a van full of young people to anywhere, and especially on such a frequent basis.

So, Sister T would soon have the key to the highway, by God's grace, and she wanted to share that grace with her instructor.

•/•

Chapter 6

*D*id you get back together with your sign all right?" Logan asked as soon as Sally stepped into the office later that day.

Oh shit. News travels fast. How am I gonna explain having a cop draw his gun on us, especially after making such a big stink about Dave?

"Yeah...it's on the back of the car again." She held her breath, waiting for the other shoe to drop.

"Look, Sal, I'm really sorry. Those magnets have been weak for a while, and I've meant to replace them. Honestly, that sign has fallen off before, only it was on a road that was under construction so it was pretty rough. But you really shouldn't have to worry about it falling off just driving through a parking lot. I called Dave, and he's going to replace them tonight."

"How did you know it fell off?"

"Oh the restaurant left a message that it came off when you pulled out."

She thought fast. They must have left the message, then talked to the cop after that. Then the cop stopped her and the kids later. Logan apparently knew nothing.

"Anyway, Gwelda was on the phones, and somehow she didn't get the message, or didn't pass it on, or something. I'm trying to work with her on multitasking, but you know, it seems like her brain just gets full. And then things start falling out. Anyway you must have gone back and got it, huh?"

"Yeah, we got it," she thanked her lucky stars. "So, what's going on with Dave, and the investigation, and everything?" A quick subject change seemed felicitous.

.⁊.

"So, it sounds like things are going all right in general, then?" Josephine was saying a couple of days later. Sally sat in her office having their meeting about the settlement proposal her almost-ex was about to make.

Sally allowed that things were okay she guessed, just the usual ups and downs at work, and she and her sister were having a disagreement. She explained about the sword.

"And which is more important to you, dear, your relationship with your sister or the sword?"

"Well, that's not the point." Sally shifted in her chair, wanting to sit up tall and indignant. "The point is, my little sister is..."

"So she's your little one, then, eh?"

"Yes and she needs..."

"...to be taught a lesson," Josephine finished the sentence.

But it sounded like she thought that was wrong, and Sally didn't want to be wrong. "Well, no, I just, she's just..."

Josephine sat quietly, calmly waiting for Sally to finish.

Dammit. Where was the doddering old woman Sally had seen fumbling around spilling coffee and making a mess at their last appointment? *I need warm fuzzy grandmotherly comfort. I've been wronged. Next I suppose she's going to expect me to accept whatever they want to give me in the divorce.* "It's the—"

"Principle of the thing?" Sally scowled as Josephine not only finished her sentence for her again, but finished it correctly. Again.

"Josephine, I spend all day teaching young people about principles, following rules, making correct decisions. I can't just toss right and wrong aside in my personal life." Sally was pretty sure she had won with that defense. She shouldn't really have to tell a lawyer about right and wrong, but she had risen to the occasion, taken the high ground. *Finish that thought, Josephine. Where's your snappy comeback now?*

Josephine seemed to be making some notes. Sally waited for her to answer, and the longer it took, the more right Sally felt. She was no fool. She'd been made a fool of many times in the past few months, but this time she was going to win one, for herself, and her dad. *Hah!*

Josephine looked up now from her papers. "Ah, yes, young people..." She sighed.

And for a moment Sally had a weird feeling she was being included in that category. But she quickly dismissed it. She was in her flipping *thirties* for heaven's sake—she'd been an adult for a long time.

"Let's say you were a young person—just hypothetically—in fact, how old were you when your daddy first promised you this sword, dear?"

"I don't know, about eight, I think." Sally tried not to let her annoyance creep into her expression, since Josephine was looking right at her. She squirmed. She felt patronized, and at the same time like she was on the witness stand.

"Uh huh. So when you were eight, if your father had said to you that you could play with the sword forever, but you could never play with your sister again—the sword, or your sister—which do you think you would have chosen?"

Sally opened her mouth to say that was just stupid, it wasn't that simple at all, but Josephine held up her hand. "I'm sorry, dear, our time is limited, and we need to move on to the settlement, which is what we came to talk about. Josephine didn't actually have the written proposal in her hands, she explained, but she had discussed with his lawyer the basic outlines of what it would be.

"I want to go over the basics with you so that you have time to think about it before the written offer comes in. Things can look a little stark in black and white legal language sometimes."

Sally nodded slowly, but was having a hard time listening because she was still fuming over Josephine's attitude about the sword. Well, she would write a letter later, and explain eloquently and in detail why she was right and Josephine was wrong about that matter. Right now she'd better listen. This was her future.

It became easier to listen as she realized that the offer Josephine was laying out sounded better than anything her other lawyer had ever discussed with her. Either her almost-ex was getting tired, which she doubted, or Josephine was a tougher negotiator than Sally would have guessed. Maybe Logan was right about her lawyering skills. Well, he had to be right about something.

"So, I've jotted down the main points, the things we just went over." Josephine handed her a piece of paper. "Take this to remind you. Mull over the general scheme of things, see if this is the kind of thing you had in mind, or that you can at least live with. Then we'll sweat out the details when we get the papers from them. Okay?" Josephine gave a quick closed-mouth smile.

Sally looked down at the paper in her hands. Her future.

"Look Sally, it sounds like you and your sister are close, and I suppose you're probably not going to lose her over this sword—although people have stopped speaking to each other for less. But to put it in poetic terms, a tarnished sword is easy to put the shine back on—a tarnished relationship, marriage or otherwise, is harder. I deal with people's tarnished relationships every day. You're losing one big relationship right now and you're going to need others to get through this. I'm not a psychologist, I'm just telling you what I know as an old lady who's been in this business for a while."

"Okay, I understand. Thank you." Sally stood and put the paper into her purse. She understood, but she still wasn't sure she agreed.

The situation with Tally nagged at her for the rest of the day, regardless of what she was doing. Given that what she was doing most of that time was working, it didn't improve her job skills.

❧

Mrs. Hanama brushed her hair at the hallway mirror. She smiled, thinking about how Sally had called the day before asking to meet at the driving school for the lesson. Sally had an appointment before it, and wouldn't have time pick her up at home as they'd planned. Mrs. Hanama watched her son Robert get his jacket on so he could give her a ride to the driving school on his way to work. This was perfect. Robert had made excuses to get out of coming along to observe on her lessons, but he couldn't refuse to give his mother a ride. This was her chance to get Sally and Robert together...

"Robert, fix that hair, it don't be sticking all out everywhere like that!"

"That's my style, ma'am."

"That no style, that a mess, go fix it, then we go." She pushed him toward the bathroom.

❧

When Sally got to the office, she went to Logan to recount her experience with Josephine. He had moved his desk to the far side of the room, so Gwelda would be nearest the door since she was supposed to be the receptionist. Gwelda was sitting at her desk with Facebook up on her computer. But she wasn't currently looking at it, because she was busy texting someone. Lying on the desk next to the keyboard was her tablet, and between texts, she was playing a game on it that appeared to involve spaghetti and monkeys somehow. Once, she picked up a paper and looked at the filing cabinet as if she might be about to take the paper over to it, but then her cellphone phone rang.

Hmm. Looks like Logan's really worked with her on multitasking. Sally walked over to Logan's desk. She needed to unload some things that she didn't especially want to share with Gwelda. While Gwelda was probably too preoccupied to care, Sally turned her back to the "reception area" anyway, and began telling Logan, in a low voice, about her problems with her sister, and Josephine's attitude toward the situation. Then she launched into her impression of Josephine's skills at negotiating.

"May I help you, ma'am?" Gwelda was now saying to someone.

"My mother needs to take a driving lesson," a male voice said.

Sally didn't turn to see who it was, but assumed someone had come in to sign his mother up for lessons. She continued talking. "So anyway, I think you're right, she is pretty good. I mean I haven't had a chance to thoroughly go over it, but..."

"What's the teacher's name, Mom...Mrs. Fender?" the male voice said.

At the mention of her name, Sally turned to see Mrs. Hanama and a twenty-something guy standing at Gwelda's desk. He looked a lot like Mrs. Hanama, but much chubbier, with short hair and thick glasses. Sally could easily see him in a bowling alley.

"Yes, that one, that one." Mrs. Hanama pointed at Sally.

"Murieta...you're here for your lesson." Sally picked up her keys and clipboard, then walked toward her student.

Mrs. Hanama put her hand on Sally's arm and turned her toward the young guy. "This my Robert we talked about." Her face glowed and her eyes darted back and forth, to one, then the other, as if that could somehow create a magical connection between them.

"Oh, hell-lo...Robert!" Inexplicably, Sally's hand went limp, and she dropped her keys. The noise as they hit the floor sparked a mental image of a ball blasting pins in all directions.

She looked at Robert, and he looked away and blushed.

Mrs. Hanama nudged her son toward Sally. He looked helplessly at his mother. "Ask her out," she mouthed, eyes blazing at him.

Sally quickly bent down to retrieve the keys as her mental image shifted to a wrecking ball blasting everything around her in all directions. A wave of horror swept over her. *Oh god. Oh god. I have to get away.* She looked toward Logan, who seemed to be enjoying this. She turned, intending to walk to Logan's desk to get her clipboard, buying time. "I need to get my clip…" She then became aware of her clipboard tucked under her arm, and looked down at it blankly. "...pen, my clip-pen, that has the clip on it, so I can clip it on my clipboard," she finished, feeling she had recovered quite gracefully. She stood at Logan's desk, hand on the edge of it, clinging as if it were a life raft.

"Looking for your clip-pen?" He held up a pen, managing to keep a straight face. "I know it's your favorite."

"Yes, yes." With sudden inspiration, she moved around the desk toward him. She laid her hand on his shoulder, then ran her fingers through his hair. "He knows it's my favorite...oh, Logan dear, you know me so well."

Logan stood. "Yes, sweetie, we are a perfect match." And he leaned over and kissed her.

Sally intended to shoot him a look that said, "You're really pushing this, butthead—back off!" But then she realized how nice the kiss was. And Logan smelled really good up this close, and...

Then Gwelda was speaking. She was actually looking up from her three-ring electronic circus and watching the action between Sally and Logan. Her mouth stopped chewing gum for a moment and spoke. "I didn't realize you two were..."

Before she could finish, Sally snatched the pen from Logan, saying quickly, and perhaps a bit loudly, "We need to get your lesson started, Murieta. Nice to meet you, Robert." Grabbing Mrs. Hanama's arm, Sally whisked her out the door.

"So sorry," Mrs. Hanama was saying. "I am not knowing about your sweetie...You should have say..."

"Oh, no, no, no." Sally said, laughing a little too much. She waved her hand to say it was nothing. "Not a problem. We're kind of on-again, off-again, anyway."

"Well next time you are being off-again, let me know, and Robert can..."

"Oh, we're pretty seriously on-again now." Sally decided to put the frosting on the cake, and keep Robert at bay permanently. "In fact, I'm pretty sure he's about to pop the question."

Mrs. Hanama looked confused for a moment. Sally pointed meaningfully to her ring finger.

"Oh...that question." Mrs. Hanama nodded slowly, with apparent mixed feelings about Sally's gain on the one hand, and her loss, or lack of it, since she would still have Robert on her hands. Then she recovered. "But do you get your divorce?"

"Oh, well, I almost have that over with, thank god. And of course Logan and I would wait a little while. But anyway, it's not for sure, I just think so." Then seeing the look in Mrs. Hanama's eyes, she added, "But I'm almost certain—it's just a matter of time."

The car they were using, Sally discovered, was low on gas. Her usual car was in the shop for maintenance, and whoever had driven this one hadn't filled it up. She didn't generally take up time on her adult drives to gas up the car. Adults generally wanted their time spent on actual driving, and could figure out things like getting gas on their own. But she might have to make an exception with Mrs. Hanama.

Maybe it was a good thing. Maybe she could use some experience in that area. Her husband didn't seem very interested in helping her learn. Would he ever show her how to gas up a car? What about Robert? Oh god, yeah, what about Robert? Her mind skipped back a few minutes to the scene at the office. Wait a minute...to hell with Robert, what about Logan? She relived that kiss for a moment...she wanted to tell Tally about it...oh yeah, what about Tally? She'd called and left several messages for her little sister with no response.

But more than all that, what about Mrs. Hanama? What was she doing? It was one those bad moments when Sally was riding along, and things were going okay, so she forgot momentarily that the person behind the wheel didn't actually know how to drive. With Mrs. Hanama, moments like that could never last very long. "Murieta," Sally said calmly, "Please don't answer your cell phone when you're driving. It's illegal, but more than that it's dangerous."

"Oh, sorry, I know, I just need to see who called. Do you think we stop by my cousin's? She has special something for Robert. His birthday is Friday."

Oh god, now I feel bad. I hope I didn't totally humiliate him. "Oh, Murieta, I'm sorry—I mean happy birthday—well I mean to Robert, of course...yes, uh, definitely no problem, we'll stop by. Is she at her store?"

"No, she's home."

"Okay, well, you'll have to show me, then." Sally shuddered at the thought of Mrs. Hanama driving and finding her way to her cousin's house at the same time. "Unless you want to give me the address and we can just GPS it."

"Oh, I don't remember her address, I just know where she's living. It's right over that way." Mrs. Hanama took one hand off the wheel to point, and they veered uncomfortably closed to a parked car which happened to be a new Mercedes.

Sally had been bringing up the GPS on her phone. "Okay," she said dubiously, looked up, and saw their trajectory. She reached over and guided them away from the parked car, which was doubly fortunate because the door was opening and someone was getting out as they passed. Sally looked right into the woman's eyes and saw fear, her face just inches away. *That could have been really ugly. But why do people ever step out in front of Driver's Ed cars anyway?*

"Both hands on the wheel, Murieta. Nine and three, remember?"

Mrs. Hanama clenched the wheel with both hands and with a look of determination made a fairly decent right turn at the next street, though she forgot to signal. Since Sally had had no idea they were turning, she couldn't remind her student of things like signaling. But Mrs. Hanama did at least seem to know where she was going, so Sally tried to relax.

She had agreed to this because she felt guilty about her charade back at the office, and she thought this was just going to be a minor detour. But soon she began to squirm in her seat, pushing her seatbelt first one way, then the other, on her shoulder. She wasn't sure where the road they were on went. Cow after cow looked up and stared at her with the same "I know exactly where I am, do you, dear?" expression. Then Mrs. Hanama turned again, onto another road Sally didn't recognize. She looked over at Mrs. Hanama, who still looked determined, but something else seemed to be creeping into her expression. "Are you still sure of where you're going, Murieta?"

"I—think—it looks—" Her brow was more furrowed, and not in a determined way. Then her face brightened and relaxed. "Oh yes, yes, yes," she said, and Sally slammed hard against her door as they made a sudden rough turn into a housing development that like the Emerald City had popped up in the middle of nowhere. This didn't look like Oz, but in spite of herself, Sally looked around for flying monkeys.

There were none, but there was also no cousin's house in sight. They meandered through the housing development, with Mrs. Hanama muttering, "Oh, yes, yes, yes" at first one street, and then another. But none of them turned out to contain her desired destination. Sally glanced over at the fuel gauge. The needle was touching "E" but the light wasn't on yet. "Murieta, let's pull over and you can call your cousin."

Mrs. Hanama nodded, then pulled over, only scraping the curb slightly. Sally could see that she was worried. Her upper lip and forehead shone with sweat.

"Good job, Murieta." Sally patted her shoulder. "I think you're really improving at that."

"Oh thank you. Robert was helping me do that by our house."

"Well, that was nice of him."

"I call my cousin now." She tried a couple of times, and left voicemails. They waited.

Sally checked her watch. She looked down the street at a couple of teenage girls walking toward them. They looked very familiar, which didn't surprise Sally, since she had seen so many teenagers that most of them looked familiar. *Wait a minute...there's something about the shine off those braces...Brittney!*

Sally rolled down her window and stuck her head out. "Brittney!"

The girls walking toward them quickened their pace. As they got closer she realized that the other girl was Carly, Brittney's usual drive partner.

"So, what are you two girls doing way out here in the sticks?"

"Sticks?" Brittney looked blanker than usual.

"Oh, I live right over there, Mrs. Fender." Carly pointed vaguely down the street.

"Oh, so you know your way around this area, Carly?"

"Yeah, pretty much."

"Well, we're kinda lost—that's why I felt like we were out in the sticks."

"What sticks?" Brittney shrugged and looked around.

"You know, like out—never mind—anyway I was about to try to GPS our way out of here, but maybe you can just point us in the right direction."

"So are you just trying to get back to town, like by the driving school?"

"Yeah, that would be great."

Carly nodded vigorously. "Oh yeah, you don't want to GPS it, Mrs. Fender, cuz it'll take you that way, right through the tulip fields and with the festival starting, all the Looky Loo's are out and it could take a while."

"Looky Loo's?" Brittney was mystified.

"That's what my dad always calls them," Carly explained. "He gets totally pissed every year. Last year, he like had a few beers, and he was out in the back yard, and all the tourist helicopters and little planes and stuff were all flying around and these two almost crashed into each other and he was like cheering and..."

"Okay, girls, that's a really interesting story and everything, but we need to get directions and get going..."

"Oh yeah, right, just go down this street, and turn left at like the first street, it's called 'Dungeness Drive.' Then just go a little ways and there's a street on the right—it's got a big rock type thingy, only it's made out of cement. I guess it's supposed to be a giant geoduck, which is some kind of clam, my mom says..." she turned to Brittney, "My dad calls it 'Dick Rock' cuz it looks just like one!" They both giggled while Sally wrote down the directions.

Carly composed herself. "Anyway you'll see it, turn there, that's the entrance to here, like our development, y' know. So then just turn left again out of here, and follow that. It winds around a lot, but it'll take you back."

"Okay, I think I've got it. Thanks, girls, see you next drive!" Sally rolled up her window. The girls waved as Sally and Mrs. Hanama pulled away.

They made their way out of the housing development. Sally's left hand quivered at the ready as they approached 'Dick Rock,' but Mrs. Hanama was able to navigate through the area without a scrape.

"So we turn left here, and that should take us back to town." Sally pointed.

"But what about my cousin? I need to get Robert's gift."

"Could Mr. Hanama pick it up?"

"Well, I think so, but I am wanting for us to talk about the flowers for your wedding, too. She would do such nice..."

"Oh, well, Murieta, that's very nice of you, but—" Sally grabbed the obvious excuse, "See the little orange light there on the dash that looks like a gas pump? We're almost out of gas, and we really have to get to a station. Besides, we're not sure where she lives, remember?"

This seemed enough to satisfy her and they continued toward town. Sally was beginning to worry about the monster she had created with her fabricated romance. She was relieved when after a few minutes, they spotted a gas station. At least that would solve her most immediate problem. She could worry about the others later.

They were about six feet away from the first pump they pulled into, so they made another pass, and almost sideswiped it. Mrs. Hanama, being small, was able to squeeze out, but was making faces like she couldn't find the gas tank. Sally found the gas card, and got out intending to show her, when she suddenly realized the gas tank on this car was on her side. Fortunately they were able get the hose to just reach. Sally showed Mrs. Hanama how to turn the pump on.

"Now just squeeze this lever. It looks like this one won't lock on, so you'll have to keep squeezing until it's full." As Sally stood waiting, she looked across the flats to the next road over, where lines of traffic crawled along by the tulip fields. Good thing they weren't out there. Though the festival wasn't yet in full swing, Carly had been right, people were apparently trying to catch a glimpse of the daffodils and early tulips before the traffic got completely gridlocked. They were creating an early traffic jam to avoid the later one. She wondered if all people ever did was solve one problem by creating another one to distract them from the first one. *Hmm. That almost sounds like something Josephine would say.*

Her thoughts were interrupted by a car pulling in at the other set of pumps. The driver turned out to be Arlene, the flower lady. Perfect. Sally could set up a time to finish their presentation plans. Maybe getting lost wasn't so bad. Things happened for a reason, and sometimes it was good.

"Hi, Arlene!" Sally walked over.

"Oh...hi..." Arlene responded sort of vaguely. It seemed to take her a minute to realize who Sally was. "Oh hi!" she said again, with much more enthusiasm. "We need to get together and finish up our work."

"Yeah, yeah, I was thinking the same thing. Would tomorrow be okay...like six-thirty or seven maybe?"

"Let's make it seven, after the tulip traffic dies down, for your sake."

"Sure, sounds good. I'll see you then." Sally heard an out-of-place noise, turned and ran back to see how Mrs. Hanama was doing.

"Oh my god," Sally breathed, as the scene on the other side of the pumps became visible. Mrs. Hanama had pulled the nozzle out, but she was still squeezing. A stream of gas was spraying out and she was standing there not moving, fingers frozen on the trigger.

"Let go, Murieta, just let go of the trigger—don't squeeze."

Mrs. Hanama apparently heard the first two words and took them literally. She let go, and the nozzle and hose clanged to the pavement.

Sally picked it up and replaced it in the pump. "What happened?" Sally said stupidly, looking at the gas all over the ground.

"I don't know...I don't know..." Mrs. Hanama kept saying.

The gas was not only all over the ground, Sally now realized it was all over Mrs. Hanama's pant legs as well. She stood next to Mrs. Hanama and patted her shoulder. "It's okay, I guess you just didn't know to let off the trigger. We'll get things cleaned up, and everything will be fine. No big deal."

"Has anyone else ever do this?"

"Oh, yeah, yeah, it happens all the time," Sally lied. She felt like she was doing a lot of lying lately. But it seemed necessary right now. "Why don't you go into the restroom and clean up as well as you can? I'll take care of this."

Mrs. Hanama headed off to get the ladies room key. Sally got a wad of paper towels, then looking down at the mess, realized that probably wasn't going to work. She pulled the car over into a spot by the store to get it out of the way then went in to see if the clerk knew what to do. When she got close to the door, which was propped open, the smell of gas fumes almost knocked her over. It seemed to have permeated the whole space inside.

"I got her out of here as quick as I could," the clerk said, "but it still reeks. Some lady somehow got gas all over her pants when she was pumping, can you believe it?"

"Oh, that's what the smell is?" Sally was rethinking the idea of asking how to clean up the gas. Maybe it would just drain away, or evaporate.

He looked out the window at her car.

"Oh, you're Driver's Ed, huh? You've probly seen everything."

"Oh-ho, yes," she laughed, "I guess I have."

He started to laugh with her, then his face changed as his eyes strayed toward the window again. She turned too and saw Mrs. Hanama getting into the car.

Busted. "I'm really sorry about the mess."

"Yeah, I'll go out and hose it off in a minute. It'll be fine. I'll enjoy the fresh air, believe me. I just wish you hadn't let her come in. Oh, here." He handed her a big bottle. "This'll be $4.95. You're gonna want the large one."

The bottle said 'professional strength' air freshener. She paid him.

"It's gonna be a long ride home."

"Okay, thanks." She grabbed the bottle and went out. As she walked over to the car, the smell was getting stronger. Mrs. Hanama had her door partway open, and the fumes were powerful enough to make Sally's eyes water as she approached.

The full impact of the situation was just now hitting her. They weren't going to leave the fumes behind in the convenience store. Mrs. Hanama couldn't wash out the smell with restroom soap.

"Roll down all the windows, Murieta," Sally said from a few feet away.

"I am trying to, but the buttons don't working. My husband's different."

"Okay, do you have the key turned?"

"Oh." She reached for the key, then her other arm moved to the door. "Won't work," She insisted.

Sally held her breath, then reached in and pressed all the buttons.

"Oh, push that way? I thought the other way." Mrs. Hanama said.

"Step out for a minute, Murieta, and let me spray some of this around," And before you get back in, I think I might have a towel in the trunk. You should probably sit on that. Also, I think whoever is picking you up should bring you some fresh clothes. You don't have to say exactly what happened, just that you spilled something. Why don't you call, while I spray?"

They drove back to the school with the windows wide open, and Sally spraying air freshener frequently and liberally. She was also hatching a plan. When they got there, Mr. Hanama was waiting in his car, looking annoyed. He rolled down the window.

Sally turned to Mrs. Hanama. "Look, Murieta, how do you want to do this? I mean, we could go in, but then we'll have to explain to everybody there, too. It might be more private for you if I just drive around back, and you change pants in the car. I can kind of stand guard, and there's usually no one back there anyway. You're pretty petite, do you think you'd have room? I mean, you can go in if you want to, but...this way you could just tell Mr. Hanama you spilled some coffee or something."

"Oh yes, yes, yes," Mrs. Hanama sounded grateful.

Sally walked over to his car. "She didn't want to get out—because of her wet clothes " She smiled. His scowl didn't change. He handed her the clothes through the window. "Murieta will be back in a minute," she said over her shoulder as she walked away.

A few minutes later, Mrs. Hanama was on her way home, and Sally was in the office, trying to figure out how to finesse the smell situation. Logan looked up from his desk and sniffed a couple of times. "Do you smell gas, Sal?"

"I don't know, maybe. Where's Gwelda today?"

"Oh, she's off. I'm not having her come in every day. I definitely smell gas." He got up and walked toward her. "There isn't a gas leak in that car is there? I can't handle any more problems with..."

She realized she had to make a decision. Tell all? Or...

"Okay, look, Mrs. Hanama had a little problem gassing up the car. I wasn't going to mention it because I didn't want to embarrass her, but..." *Or because I should have been paying attention to my job instead of talking to Arlene. But why bring that up...he's already freaked out enough about the company possibly getting shut down, I don't want him to think I'm deserting him.*

"Anyway she must have gotten a little gas on me or something." *'Or something'* seemed broad enough to include what had actually happened, which took this out of the realm of an actual lie, didn't it?

"Oh, okay, well if you have more drives today, you might want to run home and change clothes."

"Well, actually, I'm supposed to have a drive right now but it looks like a no-show, and frankly that car looked like it could use a wash, so maybe I should go get it washed and detailed?"

"Yeah, sure, Sal, what the hell. Might as well get them all cleaned up, so they're ready to sell when I get shut down." He plopped down in the chair at Gwelda's desk.

"Logan, dude, you are really down." She went over and put her hand on his shoulder.

"I tell you, Sal, sometimes life seems like this giant weird theme park. But if it were a theme park, you couldn't even give the tickets away."

Sally was in shock. "Logan, I've never heard you talk like this."

"Well, I—did you just call me 'dude'?"

"Uh, I think so..."

"When did you start saying 'dude'? There was a hint of a smile in his voice.

"I don't know.'" She laughed. "I resisted as long as I could, but I hear it all day, and I guess I finally caved, DU-U-UDE..."

He actually cracked a smile. She'd cheered him up, and it felt really good all of a sudden to cheer Logan up. She noticed then that they were smiling and looking into each other's eyes.

At that moment, Gwelda burst through the door. "Is there any chance I can get a draw? I just need enough to put gas in my..." She stopped and was now staring at them staring at each other. "Whoa! What is up with you two?"

"We were just talking about detailing one of the cars," Logan said, still looking at Sally. "I'll cut you a check. How much?" He broke their gaze, then got up and went to his desk.

"I better go get that car cleaned." Sally headed for the door.

"See you, Sal," Logan said in a tone that made her turn, and they shared a brief goodbye gaze before she went out the door.

"So you're having some like hot affair or something?" She heard Gwelda ask before the door closed.

"Or something..." Sally said softly to herself.

•/•

Chapter 7

Sally saw them pull up and ran out to greet them. "Tal! Why didn't you tell me you were coming? I've been trying to get ahold of you..."

"Oh, I meant to, Sis, that was why I called in the first place, but things were happening so fast, and then we were on our way, and I thought it would be fun to surprise you."

"But where's Nathan? Everything's okay with you guys, right?"

"Oh, yeah, yeah, Sal, more than all right—Nathan might have a job up here! Well, not right here, but like three hours away."

The girls crawled out of the car too by then and were standing on the sidewalk stretching. Sally grabbed both girls and had an arm around each. "M-m-m..." She gave both a squeeze. "It is so good to see you two. Are you excited? I am—it sounds like we'll get to see each other a lot more!"

"Now don't get too excited, it's not for sure. Nathan is over there now, for the final interview. Cross your fingers." Tally crossed hers and closed her eyes.

"Your mom is definitely excited. How about you guys? Chelsea? Zoey? Can't wait to spend more time with good ol' Aunt Sal, am I right?"

Chelsea, the ten-year-old, giggled and nodded. Zoey looked down and didn't answer.

"Zoey's busy being mad at her dad and me for probably ruining her life by moving up here."

Sally looked over at her niece. "Oh, it's tough being fifteen, isn't it, Zozo? It's so exhausting hating adults all the time. But I would think you'd want to move back home."

"Oh, she's made some new connections down there, and—"

110

"Not 'connections,' Mom, I happen to have friends, and I'd have to break up with Luis, which you'd be thrilled about..." Her hand suddenly went to her pocket, and pulled out her phone. She stared at it, then her thumbs began furiously working on the keyboard.

"Oh. I just remembered. I've got something for you." And Tally dug the sword out of the back of the van.

Half laughing, half crying, Sally hugged Tally. "You brought it!"

"Yeah, Uncle Bob didn't really care, he just thought it would look nice in his collection. He didn't have any sentimental attachment or anything. And actually you should thank Nathan, I guess. He remembered you talking about how much that old thing meant to you."

Sally knew her sister wasn't going to say, "I'm sorry, I was wrong. I understand now how much it means to you." People in movies said things like, but nobody she knew did.

Now, it was just after five and the sisters were sitting in Sally's apartment having coffee and talking.

"But Sal, he's your boss. I mean, do you think it's a good idea to get involved? And you are actually still married."

"Yeah, I know, Tal, I've been thinking all those same thoughts."

Tally's two girls were messing around on Sally's computer in the cubby hole a few feet away. The whole scene filled Sally with warm fuzzy feelings that she had been missing for quite a while. She didn't usually like surprises, but having her sister and nieces show up that morning had been a pleasant one.

Sally had gone to work and spent the afternoon in Driver's Ed World. Now she was sitting at home with her family in what felt like the real world and they were making plans for the next few days.

"I have to go see Arlene," Sally said. "So, we can have dinner, and then you guys can relax and settle in while I'm gone. It shouldn't take me very long, we just have a few loose ends to tie up."

"Okay, well, Sal, what I'm hoping is that I can leave the girls with you tomorrow while I drive over and meet Nathan. We'd kinda like to spend a day or two together, and then drive back, if that's at all possible...I don't want to ask too much, I mean I know your life is—"

"No, no, Tal, I'd love to have the girls and I'm sure you guys could use the time. Maybe you can check out the area a little. Is this a pretty sure thing?"

"Yeah, we think so. This interview is more of a formality, Nathan says."

"Well, the girls and I will have a blast. I don't have a lot of drives tomorrow because a couple of people canceled and Logan's doing one. So we'll have time to maybe do some shopping and a movie...or possibly go carts."

"Go carts!" the girls shouted in unison.

"Oh yeah, Sal, that's a good idea. Zoey is getting antsy about learning to drive."

"Hey that's right up my alley, ZoZo. Just one more reason you should be happy about moving back here."

"Yeah, I guess, but Luis said he'd teach me..."

"Is he old enough? You know, there are rules about who can ride with you when you have a permit."

But Zoey was already absorbed in the computer again.

The pizza they'd ordered arrived, and after eating her fill, Sally left to meet with Arlene. As Sally drove along, she reflected on the turn that things had taken, and she felt lighter. Things were coming around. Her family would be closer again, and that would make whatever came along easier to take.

It had begun to rain, and by the time she started up the long narrow drive to Arlene's it was getting slick with mud. She spotted an oncoming car and looked for a place to pull over. *I don't have any room, and anyway, he's coming downhill, he's required to yield.*

The other driver didn't seem inclined to move over for her, even though there was a wide spot he could have used. So she eased over as much as she could, getting over into the weeds and hoping she wouldn't get stuck. As he got closer, she got a better look at the car. *Jack!*

Her almost-ex drove past, giving her barely a glance as he sped by, nearly sideswiping her car. She let out a groan of frustration and smacked the steering wheel. Then she composed herself and pulled out.

A couple of minutes later she was walking up to the front door of Arlene's house. One of the flagstones in the walkway rocked when she stepped on it, and muddy water from beneath it shot up her pant leg. Foreboding swept through her when she looked down at the grayish brown stain. She shook off the feeling and knocked on the door. Arlene answered, but didn't step aside to welcome her in. She handed Sally an envelope. "Here's the money for the work you did on this."

"Did?"

"Yes, I've changed plans, and I won't be needing your help after all."

Sally was stunned. Then Jack's face flashed across her mind. "I just saw Jack driving away. I didn't know you knew him."

"Oh, we've known Jack for years—ever since he used to come up and work summers in the tulip fields. Well, I've got to go, dear, we're going out to dinner. Thanks for all your help, really."

Sally felt weak and sick to her stomach as she drove home. It was like her almost-ex wasn't satisfied with making her miserable just by dragging out the divorce and not giving her what was hers from their past, but now he was reaching into her life and taking away what she was building for the future.

"That bastard!" Tally said when Sally got home and told her what had happened.

"Tal, I don't know for sure that he—" A part of Sally wanted to think he hadn't done it, because then he might be out there ruining the rest of her life. She would never get away.

"Of course he did. He has always delighted in wrecking whatever you try to do, and you know it."

Tally and Sally were drinking wine on the roof. Sally's building was an old one with all the attendant architectural oddities. The front door of her apartment opened onto a small landing. The stairway down was on the right, and to the left was a gate that opened onto a flat roof. The gate was never locked, and no one had ever told Sally not to go on the roof, so she had taken to using it as her own personal deck. She had set out a couple of lawn chairs and a small table, which was where they now sat. The nieces were still inside at the computer.

"It's amazing that it didn't rain here—it was pouring over at Arlene's."

"Isn't that what they call 'microclimates,' Sal?"

"Yeah. I think Jack has his own little black 'microclimate' that travels around with him."

"Yeah, no kidding," Tally looked around, as if trying to find a something else to talk about. "Hey, you could grow some plants out here, Sal."

"Yeah, I was thinking about getting some pots and growing tomatoes, and maybe some flowers too."

The wine seemed to be mellowing them. Earlier Tally had felt strongly that they should plant a flaming bag of crap on the almost-ex's porch. They had decided that was beneath their dignity. A better idea might be to just egg his house.

Now though, they were moving on. "Maybe I'll talk to Logan about doing classroom teaching. I really feel ready now."

"You absolutely should. You'll be so great at it."

"Yeah, if I can keep from tearing Logan's clothes off in front of the class." Sally giggled, spilling her wine. Tally joined in, pounding on the little table, and the girls came out to see what was going on.

"You guys are sloshed." Zoey's voice dripped with disgust.

"Where are we sleeping, Aunt Sally?" Chelsea wanted to know.

"You gettin' sleepy, Punkin?" Tally gave her a hug, and turned with a questioning look to Sally.

"Oh, I think the girls can sleep in the bedroom, and believe it or not, there's a hide-a-bed in that loveseat in the living room for you and me. It'll be cozy, but I think it'll work."

·/·

"Wouldn't you know it would pick today not to start?" Tally looked into the mechanical abyss under the open hood of her van.

"It's probably just a dead battery, but unfortunately I think Jack ended up with all our jumper cables. You sure you don't have any, Tal?"

"I know Nathan always has some in here somewhere, but they must be in a secret compartment I don't know about, because I can't find them."

"Look, why don't you take my car? It gets way better gas mileage than yours anyway, and you don't want to take a chance on having car trouble on the way."

"Well, I...are you sure, Sis? It won't be inconvenient for you?"

"No, you can just drive me to work. I'll pick up a car and do my drives. And I can probably get Dave to look at your car." Sally was pretty sure she could just use the jumper cables from the driver's ed car to get Tally's car started, but that would be her little surprise.

"Yeah, even if we'd gotten it started, I might have had trouble down the road...it would be nice not to worry...okay, Sal, thanks a lot."

They hugged, and Sally felt like a real big sister for a change, looking out for her younger sibling the way it was supposed to be. Later Tally dropped her off at work, and as Sally watched her little sister drive away, she found herself wiping away a stray tear.

·*·

When Sally got to the office, Logan looked happier than he had for a while.

"Hey, Sal, what's up, aren't you kinda early for your drive?"

"Yeah, I was hoping I could borrow some jumper cables for my sister's car."

"Hey, I was gonna ask, did everything work out? I mean, weren't you guys having a problem?"

"About the sword? Yeah, yeah, we're great...except I think her battery is dead, and I need to get her car started, so I was hoping I could just use one of your cars and go give it a jump. She's taking my car to go east of the mountains and I'm watching her kids, so I want to get the car started so I'll have something to drive while she's gone."

"You sure it's just the battery?"

"I think so...but if it's not, is there any chance Dave could look at it?"

"Sure, sure, Sal...whatever you need...uh, by the way...can we talk soon about...you know...things?"

"I know, we need to, we will." They shared a brief look.

"Anyway, take car three, that's what you're driving today, right?"

"Thanks, Logan, I'll grab the keys."

"Oh, by the way, I won't be here most of tomorrow. Gwelda'll be holding down the fort while Dave and I go see Josephine. We're having a conference call with DOL."

"Oh, Logan, you must be worried."

"No, Sal, it's good. I think we're gonna blow 'em outta the water. Dave has really come through."

"Really?" Despite being in a hurry, Sally sat down to hear more.

"Yeah, Dave can explain pretty much everything, and from the sound of it, he really didn't do anything wrong. We're hoping we can put the whole thing to rest with this phone conference."

"Oh, Logan, that would be such a relief."

"Yeah, no kidding. Just cross your fingers, Sal."

"How did Dave explain it all?"

"Well, Dave still says he didn't call the kid a 'horrible driver' in the first place. He went back and looked at the drive sheet to refresh his memory, and he said to the kid that it was a horrible experience, but he needed to 'get back on the horse,' as a driver. He says he told the mom the same thing by phone, but the cell was cutting in and out, so he didn't know if she got it."

"Was he doing drives up in Cement Falls, or..."

"Out between Foggy Point and Chagrin Cove."

"Oh, yeah, the reception out there is terrible." Dave's story started to take on some credibility.

"He also says he went to a garage sale exactly once on a drive, because they parallel parked next to one, and one of the kids said it was his best friend's house, and could he go in and use the bathroom. Dave checked with the parent at the house, it was all good, and while the kid was inside Dave spotted a set of wheel covers that would be perfect for our cars. So he bought them. It was company business, and it was the kid's fault they were stopped there in the first place. Dave says he even got them to write a receipt, so he could get reimbursed. I actually kind of remember it myself. Anyway, Gwelda's in the back room going through receipts so we can prove it, and I'm starting to relax."

"What about going to the casino?"

"That one I'm not sure about. He says he was probably just using the bathroom or buying coffee or something..."

Yeah, "or something."

"But he's trying to pin it down to specifics. We have the date he drove with that kid on the drive sheet. Fortunately, he only drove the kid once, so we know that was the exact day."

"I'm glad it's turned your way, Logan. Good luck tomorrow. I better get going."

•/•

"Okay, girls, get ready for a fun day, I've got plans for us later," Sally said when she got back to the apartment. "I switched my schedule around so I'll just have to work for a little while this morning, and have the rest of the day with you guys. But first, we've got to work together to surprise your mom."

They followed her downstairs where she demonstrated how to hook up the jumper cables. "Okay, Zoey, hop in the driver's seat. Here's the key." Zoey's face glowed as she got in.

"Put it in the ignition." Sally stood at the open car door, watching her niece. "Now just turn it to the 'on' position, right there, to check your lights and gauges."

Zoey followed instructions. "It didn't start."

"No, it's not supposed to." Sally pointed to the various warning lights and gauges. "You look at these and make sure they're working. Then you turn it to start."

"Wow, Aunt Sally, you know a lot. Luis never—well, I don't think he does that."

Sally swelled with pride at her own knowledge. "Now, I'm going to go rev up the engine of the other car a bit and when I raise my hand, turn it to start, then let go of the key as soon as you hear the engine start. If all it does is click, or is silent, raise your hand, and I'll check the connections. Got it?"

Zoey looked up at her aunt with new admiration. "Got it."

The first time they tried, nothing happened. Sally adjusted the cables a bit then signaled Zoey. The van started up with only a little hesitation.

"Should I turn it off, Aunt Sally?"

"No, sweetie—" Sally's phone was buzzing. "Just a minute, I have to get this. It was Logan. He needed her to do a drive right away.

"Logan, I can't really, I have my nieces, and we just got the car started, and—"

"So, it's started, and you could go do the drive. The guy you need to pick up is out that way. Dave was going to do it, but Josephine needs to see us for a little while this morning to get ready for tomorrow. She said she has something important to show us."

"Well, I—I'm on kind of a tight schedule. I made plans for later."

"I really need you to do this, Sal...I'm fighting for my life here."

Sally ran it through her mind, and thought she saw a way to please Logan, be a great big sister, and an awesome aunt all at once.

"Okay, well, I guess I can squeeze it in before my other drive. But I need you to pick up the car here after I'm done today."

"Yeah, I need it up at the high school. No sweat, we'll get it. Thanks, Sal."

Sally stuck her phone in her pocket. "Okay, Zoey, we need to let it run for a while, but I have to go do a drive right now and one after that, and then we have stuff to do together. So when I get back, we'll jump it again if need be, and then you can sit in it and let it run while I change clothes and stuff, okay?"

"Yeah, definitely!" Zoey's eyes lit up. "Aunt Sally, you are so awesome!"

Sally went back upstairs, got her purse, did a quick check in the bathroom mirror, and grabbed a granola bar for the road. "I'll be back in a couple of hours."

The older gentleman she was driving with was not the best driver around, but Sally hoped that maybe a few lessons would break some of his bad habits. About halfway through the drive, though, they were stopped at a red light, and as she was making some notes on her clipboard she heard a snoring noise. She looked over and realized he was sound asleep. Sally woke him up, they switched places, and she drove him home. She made a note to have The Talk with his wife. The talk where you say it's time for him to surrender his license. On second thought, maybe she'd make Logan do it.

She had plenty of time before Mrs. Hanama's drive, so she headed home to check on the girls and the van. But when she arrived, the van was not parked where it had been. A feeling of horror mounted as she looked up and down the street for it. It was nowhere in sight. She called the police, who assured her that the car had not in fact been stolen, but was being towed from the crash scene where her niece had apparently run off the road.

"Oh my god! Is she all right?"

"Yes, ma'am, but the car might not be. They're busy getting it towed from the crash scene right now. "

"Was she alone, do you know?"

"Uh yes, ma'am. The officers should be there with her shortly."

In shock, Sally dashed upstairs to make sure Chelsea hadn't been kidnapped or something. On the way, she tried to figure out a way to keep Tally from finding all this out. She was pretty sure this wasn't her fault, but was equally sure Tally would think it was.

Chelsea was fine, had fallen asleep watching TV. She confessed that she and her sister stayed up late talking the night before. She was clearly oblivious to the disaster taking place below. "Where's Zoey? She stretched and yawned.

Sally tried to come up with one of the impromptu lies she had been so good at lately. "Maybe she fell asleep in the car, huh?" They both laughed, but Sally's laugh was thin and high.

"Oh, yeah, she probly did. She went down to get some of her stuff after you left."

"Wait a minute, how did she get in the car? I had the keys." Sally started checking her purse.

"She said you left some on the bathroom counter for us in case we needed to get in."

The keys did not seem to be in Sally's purse. *Oh god. I came up and went in the bathroom. I had the van keys in my hand and I decided to brush my hair. I might have...did I really...did I really set them on the counter? Then I grabbed the car keys from my purse, so thought I had...oh it's this stupid job, I just have too many sets of keys. But...Tally will kill me. And Zoey.*

When the police pulled up, Sally was standing next to Logan's car, waiting. She could see one officer poke the other, then point.

"This yours?" The officer nearest her asked as he got out, pointing to the Driver's Ed car next to her. They could barely suppress their laughter when she confirmed that it was. Sally mentally ran through the top ten worst moments of her life, and penciled this in somewhere around four.

"You the mom?" the older cop asked.

"No, the aunt." Sally had a creeping suspicion that she'd seen this older guy before. *Oh god. The sign. He's the cop that...*

He was looking at her a little more intently. "Aren't you the lady...?"

"Yes." She nodded. "I'm that lady."

His partner looked at him quizzically. "She works for Logan. Tell ya about it later," the older guy muttered. He turned again to her. "Never a dull moment in Driver's Ed, eh?" He half-smiled and the skin at the corners of his eyes crinkled.

He knows Logan? I wonder if he told Logan about the whole sign back story? "No, not many."

"So you're her aunt, you said?"

"Yes. Her mom is out of town. I'm taking care of her and her sister."

119

"Well, she went for a little joy ride, and put the car in a ditch. It was out in the county, so the county sheriff'll be sending her a citation." He opened the back door to let Zoey out.

"They told me she's okay, is the car damaged?" Sally hadn't called Tally yet. She was waiting to see how bad the damage was. She was crossing her fingers and praying, although she wasn't at all religious, except at times like this.

"Well, the right side is pretty bashed in," the younger cop said. "She really did a number—"

"But it looked drivable to me," the older man broke in, with some sympathy in his voice. He probably had kids.

Zoey was now out of the car, and tried to brush past without a word. Sally grabbed her arm. "We need to talk."

Zoey scowled and stood with her arms crossed, staring at the ground.

"Anything else, officers?"

"Just sign here. And here, take this to pick up the car at the tow yard." He handed her a piece of paper. They waved as they walked toward the car. She winced when she saw them laughing as they drove away.

Zoey was still standing with her arms folded but now she was staring and making a face at her sister who was at the bottom of the stairs watching the police drive away.

"How come the police were here?"

"Oh, I'll explain later, Chels. Right now I need you to go back upstairs and see if I left my cell phone laying around somewhere, okay?"

Chelsea trotted dutifully up the stairs, and Sally turned to Zoey.

"What?" Zoey said in her snottiest tone.

"That's what I thought I'd ask you, Zoey. I'm pretty hurt right now, to tell you the truth. I accidentally left the keys and you took advantage. Now we're both in trouble. What were you thinking?"

"Luis called after you left, and his dad had a heart attack, and he was so scared and everything and I just wanted to be with him."

"You thought you were going to drive to California?"

"Yes! No—I don't know. I just wanted everything to be different!" she wailed, and ran up the stairs.

Now I remember why I never had kids. What next? Sally went upstairs to find that Zoey was in the bathroom, crying. Chelsea was in the kitchen nook making a sandwich.

"I couldn't find your phone, Aunt Sally."

"What? Oh, Chels, I actually had it, I just needed to talk to Zoey alone." When she saw the look on Chelsea's face," Sally added, "I know, Chelsea, I shouldn't have, I was just in a hurry. I'm sorry."

"It's okay, Aunt Sally." Chelsea gave Sally a big hug, which reminded her how much she missed having her nieces around. Nobody hugged with the same enthusiasm and sincerity as a kid. "What's going on, anyway, Aunt Sally?"

Sally explained briefly what had happened.

"So, you want me to keep things on the D.L., when mom comes?"

Sally laughed. "I'm going to call your mom, so, no, you won't need to keep things on the 'downlow.'"

Sally called Logan. To her great relief, Logan smoothed the path to getting the car back. They were done at Josephine's, and things were apparently looking really promising. Their conference call with DOL would be at four that afternoon, and Logan was feeling confident.

As it happened, Dave knew the guy who ran the towing yard, and headed right out to see how bad the car was. He said maybe he could pop it back into shape somewhat, so it wouldn't look quite so bad when her sister got back.

Zoey needed to be dealt with in some way. Sally took a deep breath, then went in and found that her niece had stopped crying, and was sitting quietly on the floor. Sally stroked her hair. "So, are you okay? You don't have a sore neck or any aches and pains?"

"No, I'm okay, I guess. I just wish none of this would have happened."

"I agree. But it didn't just happen. Car crashes don't just happen accidentally, even though people call them 'accidents.'"

"So cars don't kill people, people kill people?" Zoey smirked.

"Yeah, something like that. And you could have killed yourself or someone else today."

"I might as well be dead if I'm stuck here and Luis is in California."

"Zoey, you know better than that."

"Well, Mom is gonna kill me anyway, so what difference..."

"You and your mom have some talking to do. I'm just here to say that this was irresponsible, and it will be a long time before you can get a license because of what you did today."

"Yeah, I get that. Sorry..." Her eyes brimmed with tears.

"I still love you, y'know?" Sally put her arm around Zoey's shoulder and gave her a squeeze. "Oh, and you need to talk to Chelsea."

"Chelsea?"

"Yeah, explain why what you did was wrong, and that she better not ever pull anything that dumb. Be a big sister. And get yourself together, we're going to go have some fun in a little while."

Sally went out on the roof to think. Checking her watch, she mulled over how long she could wait to call Tally. *Oh god, Mrs. Hanama's drive! Yeah, I'm late.* She called and apologized, then rescheduled it to Monday. She was just finishing up with that when a call came in from Josephine.

Josephine had arranged a meeting with the almost-ex and his attorney for Monday, she said.

"Uh well, that's just a couple days away, and I have a lot going on." Sally couldn't believe all of this was happening at once. But the appointment time was right after Mrs. Hanama's drive. She could make it work.

"I know it's quick, but it's either that or in another month. Supposedly those are the only two times that will work for them. I think they're messing with us. But I didn't think it could happen too quickly for you."

"I know, I know. It's just that the way things are going, I'm afraid I'll be an innocent victim of blind justice." Sally tried to laugh.

"Oh, I've spent many years practicing law as you know, and believe me, justice isn't blind, my dear," Josephine said.

Before Sally could protest, Josephine finished,"...it's crosseyed. So, are you in for the meeting?"

Sally still wasn't quite sure how to take Josephine sometimes. "Yeah, I'm in." *I don't exactly have a good feeling about this, but I might as well get it over with, and move on.*

"Now, I want to warn you ahead of time—I'm gonna goof on 'em a little bit."

"Goof on 'em?" Sally remembered goofing on adults when she was a kid, but...

"Yeah, it's one of the things you can look forward to when you're old. You get to goof on younger people. Anyway, I'm going to act kind of doddering and out of it at first, so they'll get sloppy and I can take advantage of them. Okay?"

"Okay," Sally was beginning to see what Logan meant about her lawyer.

The conversation ended, but before she could get her phone back into her pocket, a text came in from Dave. Attached were pictures of the van. She peeked at the caved-in side of it in the first photo. Her heart fell. She called her sister. After she assured Tally that everybody was okay, and the car was probably at least drivable, Tally said she'd call back. She was over halfway there at this point, and felt she should talk to Nathan about how to plan things. Her parting words were, "I don't know who to be madder at, my daughter or my sister."

Sally was desolate. She consoled herself that she would get enough money in the settlement to help pay for the damage to the car.

She had been looking forward to all the fun she and the girls would have, and how excited they would be when she presented them with the trampoline. But now she felt like her trampoline had lost all its bounce. She was pulled out of her funk by a horn honking. She went to the window, and saw the van pulling in. It looked like Logan was at the wheel. She could only see the front of it, which looked all right. "I'm going downstairs for a minute to talk to my boss, girls. You just hang out here. Okay?"

Sally felt another level of dread with each step down the stairway. When the van finally came into view, she thought she must be looking at the wrong side. *But it was supposed to be the passenger side, she went into the ditch, that's the side it should be.*

"Logan? Is this? Where's the big—"

"The big giant dent?"

"Uhhh...yeah..."

"Dave fixed it. He popped it out, and put a little touch up paint on the scrapes. My brother's a genius at this kind of stuff. I mean it's not perfect, if you stand and look from this angle," Logan moved a couple of feet and cocked his head, "you can see it's still there, but it's way better than it was."

Sally just stared. Was it possible? She took her phone out to compare the picture Dave had sent earlier. Logan looked over her shoulder. "It's amazing," Sally marveled.

"I know, right?" Logan agreed.

Sally had an impulse to hug him, and followed through on it.

"Wow, I'm glad I delivered the car instead of having Dave do it!"

"This is just so awesome. I know Tally isn't going to be thrilled or anything, but this is so much better than what I prepared her for I don't think she's going to kill me, either. What can I do to thank Dave?"

"Maybe just bake him some cookies. Oh, and be extra nice to Gwelda—she keeps telling Dave she doesn't think you like her, and it hurts her feelings."

"Done and done!"

"And you could give me the key to my car. I 've gotta go do a couple of drives before our rendezvous with DOL. Remember I took one of your drives so you could play with your nieces?"

"Oh, Logan, I'll make you some cookies too."

"How 'bout a massage too? My neck is pretty kinked up from all the stress of this meeting..."

"Yeah, right...I'll go get the keys." She turned and went up the stairs feeling lighter with every step. She called Tally, who wasn't answering. She left a message that Dave had done some straightening, and safety-checked the car, and it was safe to drive.

Sally decided they should get out and enjoy the tulip festivities, so she took the girls to a famous tulip garden that had every color and variety including ones that looked black, and some that didn't even look like tulips. To her relief, the girls were impressed. Zoey got over her pouting, and Sally managed to forget about the fallout she had left to deal with. They all relaxed and enjoyed themselves. Then they went to the street fair and bought T-shirts and other souvenirs.

Surprised she hadn't heard from her sister, Sally checked her phone and discovered a missed call. The voice mail said they were on their way back over. Nathan had gotten the job. They were leaving for California as soon as they got back and got everything packed into the van. Sally couldn't tell for sure how angry Tally might be at this point. She would have to wait until they got back.

The traffic was horrible, so they walked to a burger place Sally knew about for dinner. It was absolutely packed when they got there, and Sally hoped the girls would be entertained by the novelty of the place. It had an old fashioned railroad theme and the food was actually delivered to the tables by a model train. Sally watched the girls watch burgers and shakes come around the curve on a flatcar. She had been worried they were too old to enjoy this. But Chelsea's eyes lit up, and Zoey watched too until her gaze strayed to a couple of boys at another table. Then her eyes lit up too and Sally felt like she'd picked the right place. The food, when it arrived, was great and they all were full, happy, and a little bit sleepy by the end of dinner.

As they were leaving, Sally's phone buzzed in her pocket. It was a text from Tally, but she had also apparently missed a call from Logan earlier. Tally and Nathan had made a couple of extra stops, were now stuck in the tulip traffic and would be later than planned. They would probably spend the night at Sally's, and leave early in the morning.

When Sally and the girls got home, she got them set up to watch a movie online. Then she sat down to call Logan.

"So, what's up, du-u-de..."

"Well, you're in a good mood, Sal."

"Yeah, the girls and I have had a fun day. Well, except the first half..."

"Have you talked to your sister?"

"Briefly, and it wasn't too good."

"Aw, you'll work it out—you're sisters. And it isn't like it was your fault or something."

"I did leave the keys laying around."

"Keys don't wreck cars—"

"People do. I know, I know."

"Anyway, I had an all-good day."

"So the conference call went well?"

"Oh, did it ever. Josephine kicked butt."

"Logan, I'm so happy for you. So it's all behind you now?"

"Yeah, Dave and I are having a couple of beers to celebrate. Listen, it's getting kind of loud in here, Sal. What I wanted to see about was, well, if we could maybe have dinner tomorrow night. We said we'd talk, and we haven't yet. Besides I want to regale you with the whole story of our glorious victory today. What do you say?"

"Well, I have to get ready for my big meeting Monday, and..."

"Come on, Sal, you don't have to spend every minute on that, and you know you want to hear all the details about today..."

"Well, okay, I guess just dinner maybe."

"Great. Señor Szechuan's?"

"Yeah, Logan, that sounds good."

•⁄•

Margo E. Peterson

"Come on girls, let's get your stuff out of the bedroom and take it downstairs." Nathan got up from breakfast at Sally's miniature table the next morning. He turned toward Sally and Tally. "I'm sure you two want to talk. No fistfights, or clawing, please." He chuckled and threw his hands up as if warding off their blows.

Sally laughed with him. She liked Nathan, and knew his kidding was good natured. It was his way of reminding them not to get carried away, to remember their sisterly love. Sally watched him walk away, and he looked like the perfect man. She wondered if her sister realized how lucky she was to have his sweet nature, and intelligent good looks all to herself.

He and Tally had gotten in late the night before. They had stopped for dinner to wait out the traffic, taken a romantic tiptoe through the tulip fields and ended up getting in after Sally and the girls had gone to bed.

Sally turned back toward her sister. "So do you want me to wait to mention the trampoline?" Sally mouthed the word 'trampoline' soundlessly since the girls were in the next room.

"Yeah, Sal, we don't have room. Just make it a 'welcome back' gift."

"That's a good idea."

Nathan and the girls came through with their bags just then. "We'll be back. Might be a few minutes, since I think Zoey and I want to have a little talk, don't we, Zo?"

Zoey rolled her eyes as she came through, pulling her bag along. Chelsea covered her mouth to suppress a giggle as they went out the door.

Tally looked intense. "Sally, how did this happen? How did you let her get out in the car like that? She could have been killed."

"She's sixteen, Tally, don't you think you should be putting some responsibility for this on her?"

"She's just a kid, she's upset about the move and everything—"

"Look, I've talked to other people about this, and they don't see it as my fault."

"People? Who? People who have kids...or Logan?"

"Well, Logan, for one."

"And how many kids does Logan have?"

It occurred to Sally then how much her little sister sounded like their mother. "Well, hundreds, actually. He helps mentor hundreds of teens into adulthood every year."

Tally looked annoyed.

126

"Tal, I know you're usually on top of these things and I'm the screw up. And I'm not a mom, but as a driving instructor, I think you have some blind spots you might need to check, where your daughter is concerned."

"Oh, really, well I'll be the judge of what I need to do for my daughter."

"Tally, you sound exactly like Mom."

All at once Tally's face lost its confident composure, and Sally thought she was about to cry. "Don't say that. Just don't." She took a sip of coffee, to steady herself, it seemed. "I had a call from the Gardens—you know, where Mom lives."

"Is she okay, Tal?" Sally reached over and laid her hand on Tally's shoulder.

"Oh, yeah, she's just flipping out again. It wears on me. I'm stressed, Sal. Nathan and I stopped to look at a possible place for her to live up here. That's one of the things that delayed us. We talked about Zoey, too. I know we need to do some work with her. I—I'm just stressed, Sal."

Sally knew that "I'm stressed" meant "I'm sorry" in their brand of Sisterese, and it was close enough for her.

She saw Tally and the family off later that morning. They promised to let her know when they got safely home.

As she hugged her sister, Sally said quietly in her ear, "Maybe we can find a place for Mom that's somewhere between your house and mine, and I'll really try to be more help, okay?"

Tally gave her an extra squeeze. "Thanks, Sal. That would be great."

•/•

"Yeah, I'm tellin' ya, Josephine knew exactly what to do," Logan was saying over dinner that evening. "She made a tape of Dave saying the kid's drive was a horrible experience, but he should get back on the horse as a driver. And she had a bunch of like scratchy background noise, and then she cut out words and parts of words out, like on a cellphone." Then she said it was a simulation, and asked the woman if she could have possibly misunderstood, because of all the interference.

"I wouldn't have thought she'd be so good with electronic stuff."

"Josephine? Oh she's not, believe me. Gretchen, her assistant, did it. She's really tech savvy. Josephine just came up with the idea. That's what she's so good at."

"Well, obviously it worked."

"Yeah, and we shot 'em down on the garage sale thing. We had a receipt, and an affidavit saying the woman remembered the kid coming into the house to use the bathroom. And the whole casino thing was that Dave went in to use the restroom, and while he was in there this woman came over and gave him a check for a no-show fee she owed for her daughter. One of the busybodies saw it, and thought he was getting a payout for winning. In short, it was all crap."

"I'm really happy for you, Logan. I know how this has weighed on you."

"Hey, I just hope things go as well for you on Monday. With Josephine in your corner, I'm sure they will, too, Sal." He reached across the table and laid his hand over hers. "We said we'd talk."

"I know...and I'd like to have something definite to tell you...but there are all these things..."

"All what things?"

"Well, I mean, you're my boss, and I'm still officially married, and..."

"Yeah, yeah, I know, but...well, I guess I need to know, do you want to find a way, or are you just building up a wall of details to stop it?

Jeez, Logan. I didn't expect you to be so direct, and make so much sense. Why do I always underestimate you? "I like you, Logan, maybe more than I want to at this exact time in my life, but there's definitely something—"

She was about to say "between us" when a piñata fell and landed on the table—between them, sending salsa and nachos flying.

They both looked up at the ceiling, as if it might be raining piñatas, and they should check to make sure they weren't about to get hit in the head with the next one.

Logan regained his presence of mind first. "You're okay, right? You didn't get hit in the eye with hot salsa, anything?" As she nodded, he summoned a waitress to clean things up,

Sally stared at the piñata. "What is that supposed to be?"

"A fortune cookie. What did you think it was?"

"A bedpan," She blurted out, covering her mouth as she giggled.

He began laughing along with her, and by the time the waitress got there they were both helpless. Dinner proceeded in the same lighthearted vein, and the thread of their serious conversation was lost. Later, on the way home, Logan picked it up again as he turned onto the road that led to her apartment. "So due to the, uh, 'fortuitous' arrival of the cookie, we didn't really finish our talk."

She bopped him on the arm for the bad pun.

"Hey, you're messing with my driving!"

"No, I'll show you messing with your driving!" She slammed on the dual brake.

"Very funny, Sal. Let up now, there's a car coming."

She checked the instructor mirror. "No there's not." There's zero traffic on this road in the evening.

"Okay, so I guess that's just what I get for driving an instruction car. Was that just a joke, or are you saying you're putting the brakes on 'us'? Is that the message, Sal?"

"No." She let up on the brake, and he gave it some gas. "I just need to…" She braked, more smoothly this time, but the engine revved as he kept his foot on the gas.

"I thought that wasn't good for the brakes, Logan, that's what you teach in class, isn't it?"

"Oh, so you're paying attention to me then, huh? Maybe you should start teaching classes."

She let off the brake and the car shot forward.

"We need to get some rhythm going here, girl."

"Well, I told you I wanted to start teaching classroom."

"Classroom is hard, Sal. You have to be ready for it. I don't want you to have a bad experience."

"So you're trying to protect me? Yeah, well that sounds just like my almost-ex-husband, always keeping me from achieving anything real in life because he was supposedly protecting me from the mean ol' nasty world! Well I'll tell you what, dude, I don't need anybody's protection—I've got my sword and I'm gonna wield it—"

Sally wasn't really sure where she was going with that, but she was saved from finding out when Logan leaned over and kissed her. She kissed back, but then feeling like she was in some old Hollywood movie, pulled away. "You've got to stop doing that. It's—oh shit!"

She pushed the brake down. She had forgotten about it while they kissed, and they had been rolling along at about five miles an hour. She was about to finish explaining to him when the inside of the car was bathed in red and blue light. "Okay, we need to pull over. I'll let off the brake, you steer right."

She relinquished control, letting Logan pull over to the curb. In her mirror, she watched the cop get out and walk up to their car. *Oh god. Is he the only cop in this town?*

It was Officer Pick-Up-the-Drivers-Ed-Sign-and-Bring-Zoey-Back-From-Crashing-the-Car.

"Oh, hi, Logan," he said through the open window. "I was just going to tell you your right brake light is out. I thought it was a student because of the way you were driving."

"Oh, yeah, we were just—"

"Testing the brakes," Sally finished for him.

"Yeah, I think they're okay, don't you, Ms. Fender?" Logan turned to Sally.

"Yeah, I think so."

"Well, this is a pretty quiet street, but still somebody could be right behind you. You should really do that sort of thing in a dark parking lot, you know?"

"Uh, yeah, Chester, thanks, I'll take that under advisement."

The cop put his hand on the brim of his cap, "G'night, Logan…Ms. Fender." His eyes sparkled and the skin at the corners began to crinkle.

What? Is this Andy of Mayberry, or something?

As he turned to walk back to his car, she knew his face was breaking into a grin.

*This is just like Jack. Logan knows everybody here, because he grew up around here, and they are all just making a joke of my life. That's what my almost-ex and his lawyer will do on Monday, and that's what Logan is doing now. Even if I finally get free of Jack, I'll probably marry Logan and then I'll be stuck as a driving instructor and have three screaming kids and…*Maybe she'd had too much wine at dinner, but it all just seemed too much, an endless pattern. Sally dissolved into tears.

"Oh god, Sal…because we got stopped by a cop? I mean, it didn't matter…"

Through the blur of her tears, Logan looked completely miserable and helpless. "I need to go home," she said between sobs. "We can talk after Monday. There's been too much—I'm all—"

"Well, yeah, I guess a lot's happened in the past couple days. I get it, Sal." He started the car and they drove home in silence, save for her intermittent muffled sobs.

Chapter 8

*A*fter brushing her hair, Sister T dressed and put on her robe to get ready for her bus ride downtown. She felt confident that this would be one of her last rides. Soon, with the help of her instructor, she would be at the wheel, with a license in her pocket. She was sure she had only hit those bushes last time because her hood had blocked her vision. With Brother's blessing, today she was going to buy some suitable driving clothes.

•⁄•

Brushing her hair at the bathroom mirror, Sally smoothed her bangs, then mussed them a bit with her fingers, then smoothed them, and mussed again…trying not to contemplate the prospect of sitting down face to face with her almost-ex. She had made careful plans to be sure she would get there early so she and Josephine could talk things over first. She would be dropping Mrs. Hanama at the bowling alley, which was only a couple blocks from Josephine's office. Mrs. Hanama had arranged for her husband to pick her up there. While she was worried, because Jack always seemed to find a way to turn the tables on her, she did have a feeling that things were falling into place for real this time. There was a sense of finality in the air.

She had decided this was a good day for Mrs. Hanama to do a country drive. That would be the best bet for a low stress day. Not that she was especially good at country driving, with the frequent curves and higher speeds, but there was just less traffic and less in general to hit out there. Sally wanted to keep her adrenaline level low. She visualized walking into

Josephine's office, calm and confident. They would hammer out the details, and it would be over, leaving only the formality of finalizing it in court. *My almost-ex will soon be my ex, once and for all.*

She looked out the window. It was a beautiful day, perfect for a country drive. Maybe they would even cruise along Geoduck Drive…well, that might be pushing it. Extreme curves on a cliff overlooking the Sound, one misjudgment possibly landing them in the bay…no, maybe not. She didn't feel like practicing emergency procedures for escaping a submerged car. Mrs. Hanama's husband could teach her that some other time. Sally just needed to coast today.

Maybe Clearmud Road? Yeah, that's just the place. Almost no traffic out there—not much to go wrong. She brushed her teeth, She smoothed her bangs again. She went over the papers Josephine had given her.

Later they cruised along Clearmud Road, the windows open because the air conditioning would only blow warm air for some reason. Sally would have to tell Logan. But they were only going about thirty-five, and the breeze felt good. Sally was enjoying the scenery and Mrs. Hanama was actually keeping the car on the road. Maybe all the lessons were finally paying off. Maybe…*Oh my god! Is that her? Sister T? Oh no. It is. The Grim Reaper!*

They were driving by the old abandoned mission which was now apparently not abandoned, from the general activity there. The familiar dark figure stood at the bus stop in front of it.

Oh, this can't be good. Sally began to get the jitters about the whole day. Things were going the wrong way. They needed to get off this road.

"I have to tell you something." Mrs. Hanama turned to look at Sally. Apparently this was important.

"Okay, but look at the road, Murieta."

"My cousin is winning some money on the lotto ticket I was supposed to give you."

"WHAT? *My* ticket was a winner? I'm a millionaire?"

"Oh, no, no, no…"

"What do you mean, no?"

"She only match some numbers, not all. She don't tell me how much money, but I told her she has to share with you, or I won't speak to her. I tell her I know you would if the ticket I give you won. You would be honest."

Sally couldn't think of a response to that, but she felt her luck had changed, Grim Reaper or not. Things were going to be fine. She had some money coming. Maybe she didn't have to worry so much about how much she got at the meeting.

Sally dug in her pocket for her phone. She wanted to see how much money you could potentially win by only matching up some of the numbers. There must be something about that at their website. "Okay, Murieta, turn right up here." Sally pointed toward the highway.

"Right here?" Mrs. Hanama asked, as Sally searched for the website.

Sally was pitched almost into Mrs. Hanama's lap by the hard right turn, then back to her seat, the side of her head slamming against the door post as the car lurched and jolted over the rough terrain. Just as Sally recovered and was about to take control, something jabbed through the window, knocked her phone from her hand, and snapped her in the face. Her face stung, but her hand stung more from the bee that had also come through the window. Little yellow flowers littered her and the car. They were driving through a field of scotch broom. Sally got her foot back onto her brake, and slammed it down. When they came to a stop, she yanked the parking brake, and shifted into park.

Sally sat silently, catching her breath, and assessing the situation. All around them long dark green fingers adorned with garlands of canary-yellow flowers reached toward the sky. The breeze kicked up again, and the dark fingers began to wave.

"Murieta..."

"You say turn."

"I meant at the highway, not the vacant lot."

"Oh. I wonder."

"Are you okay, Murieta?"

"Oh, yes, yes, yes...but you are not looking so okay. Your face red."

Sally checked in the visor mirror. Her face had a red streak across it from getting smacked with the branch. Her hand seemed to be swelling from the bee stings. Overall, she was not so okay, and was pretty sure she should call Josephine and cancel the meeting. But her phone was nowhere to be found. She looked under and behind both seats until her head and neck began to ache. She sat down again in the passenger's seat. Mrs. Hanama stood outside, staring at the scotch broom and muttering something in a foreign language, presumably her native Tagalog. "Murieta, I need to use your phone, if that's okay."

"Yes okay, but my husband is keeping it. I use too many minutes on calls to my family back home, and he is saying it's too expensive."

There was no way to call and cancel. Everything was lining up to make this meeting happen. It must be written in stone somewhere. She just hoped it wasn't her tombstone.

They set about pulling scotch broom branches and flowers from the car, brushing themselves off, and arranging their clothes and hair. Sally checked around and under the car. It looked okay, she guessed, so she drove it out onto the shoulder of the road. Fortunately, the ground was dry. Had it been raining they probably would have been stuck in the mud. Sally wondered though if that might have been better.

She debated with herself about doing the rest of the driving too, but her sore neck and headache were getting worse, not to mention the bee stings on her hand. She had never been stung by a bee before, and hadn't realized how much it hurt. As she was opening the first aid kit in the trunk to look for some kind of bee sting stuff, she cut her other hand on the edge of the case. That seemed like a really bad design for a first aid kit.

While she hadn't minded pulling the car out of the field, she decided she didn't feel like driving all the way back. She figured Mrs. Hanama had made her big booboo for today, and the ride home could be uneventful. The way her head throbbed, she began to wonder if she had a concussion. She thought about taking a migraine pill, but she didn't think you were supposed to take anything if you had a concussion. Besides that might be taking things a little too much for granted with Mrs. Hanama's driving.

They just needed to get back to town, and she would tell Josephine she couldn't possibly do this today. She had probably been saved from another horrible experience with her almost-ex. This hadn't been fun, but things happened for a reason. *Although, winning money on the lotto ticket is a good omen. Maybe I should go. Or maybe…with the lotto money, I won't need money from the divorce. I don't need the meeting today…I can delay it.* She was torn.

．ſ。

135

Sister T stood on the corner waiting to cross. As she looked across the street to the clothing store, a car with a sign on it came into view. A sign! Yes it was, surely God's confirmation. It was her driving instructor's car approaching the intersection. Sister T waved to her, trying to get her attention.

•/•

Traffic was backed up. When they moved it was at a crawl. Sally began to believe that she would get there too late, and everything would already be decided without her. Josephine would put on her senile act, and the men would take complete advantage of her before she knew what happened. Jack would win, and Sally would be out of luck, and then the lotto ticket would turn out to be a $10 winner and…

"How many numbers did she match, Murieta?"

"She not telling me."

Finally, they got to the source of the hold up in traffic. A bus full of tulip tourists had broken down, and was parked halfway into the road. The tourists were busy taking pictures of the bus and each other, and the traffic, and anything else they could find, since there weren't any tulips here.

The driver was flagging traffic around the bus. He waved Mrs. Hanama on, and soon they were moving full speed again. Sally checked her watch. They could still make it. Maybe.

They were getting close to Josephine's office. Her headache had started to subside. Maybe she would go through with the meeting. She was injured; she would have sympathy on her side. As they approached the intersection, she struggled to decide. They could go right to drop off Mrs. Hanama as planned and then Sally would drive to Josephine's for the meeting. Or go left, and Sally would go into Josephine's just long enough to cancel the meeting, then drop Mrs. Hanama off, then go home and have several glasses of wine. Sally's eye was caught just then by the same dark shadowy figure that had been waiting at the bus stop out on Clearmud Road. *Oh god, the grim reaper is waving at me...*

•/•

Mrs. Hanama felt terrible about turning through the scotch broom into the vacant lot, but she had thought she saw a driveway. She had wanted to do an especially good job today. Robert helped her practice the day before, and he said, "I think you're doing better, Mom." She, too, felt she was improving.

And she wanted to do well today partly so Sally could relax. She knew it was a big day for her instructor. But she had worries of her own. Mr. Hanama had been pushing her to stop her driving lessons. He was tired of paying for the lessons and had become convinced that she would never learn anyway. So Robert had started helping her. He was a good son, he really was.

Now she heard Sally say to turn. She was pretty sure her instructor had said to turn left, but then she was saying to turn right, and who was that lady in black waving at them?

Now Sally was shouting "STOP!" Mrs. Hanama got more confused by the second...

·/·

The Grim Reaper kept waving. Rattled, Sally looked first left, then right. *Okay, I have to decide. I'm confusing Murieta, and that is not a good—*

The shape flashed in front of them, seeming to shoot straight out of the Grim Reaper. Sally screamed "STOP" and hit her brake at the same time, but before the car stopped there was a sickening thud. As the car came to rest, so did her almost-ex, sprawled across the hood, his face staring up at her.

She couldn't actually tell if his eyes were open or closed because he was wearing his usual mirrored sunglasses.

·/·

Sally was mad at Logan because the brake hadn't worked, and she assumed it was because he hadn't made sure it got the proper maintenance. Logan was mad at Sally because he was pretty sure that hitting a pedestrian was going to adversely affect the reputation of the "Nash No Crash Academy." Logan was mad at Dave because maintaining the brakes was his job. Dave was mad at Gwelda because it was her job to pass along messages when the cars needed work. Mr. Hanama was mad at Mrs. Hanama because he had told her she should give up on her driving lessons, and now Look What Happened When She Didn't. Nobody really knew if the almost-ex was mad at anybody, because as far as anyone could find out, he lay in the hospital with tubes and monitors hooked up everywhere.

Sally moped around the apartment. "Around" was the right word, since the apartment was so small that any moping had to be done in circles. She called Tally for moral support.

"What if he dies? I mean, he was—is—a jerk, but I never hated him enough to want anything like that. I just wanted a divorce."

"I know, Sal, I know."

"If he does die, though…oh god Tal, what if I'm charged with murder? I could end up in prison. My life is over."

"Calm down. You're not charged with anything yet. Anyway, it would probably just be manslaughter."

"Oh good, now I feel better. Just manslaughter. Actually, as a driving instructor, I believe it would be charged as vehicular homicide." Sally felt momentarily bolstered by her expertise in the matter.

"You weren't even driving. I don't think you can be held responsible. And from what you said, the witnesses all agreed he ran out into the street against the light. Why don't you call Josephine and ask her about the legalities?"

Sally had already thought of that, but when she called, Josephine was in a meeting with Logan, increasing Sally's paranoia about getting hung out to dry for this.

"Yeah, I did that, but she was busy talking to Logan."

"Okay, well, look, Sally, while you wait just don't get yourself all wound up. Things have a way of working themselves out."

It was just the sort of thing people were always saying to Sally that drove her absolutely bonkers. What in the hell did any of that really mean, anyway? Things did always work themselves out, but often they worked out so that somebody was dead or in prison, and in this situation a little of both was possible. Tally might as well have said "it is what it is." That had been her almost-ex's answer to almost everything and it meant almost nothing to her. As someone who hoped to possibly teach English someday, she felt that people should be required to use words that had actual meaning. "Define 'it!' Define 'is!'" She always wanted to scream when someone said "it is what it is" to her.

The conversation ended, and Sally tried to hit the button on her cell phone in some satisfying way, but it was impossible. She longed for the kind of heavy two-piece phone they had in old movies. Slamming that sucker down would be satisfying. She threw her phone at the couch, where it disappeared behind the cushions.

Throwing the phone made her neck hurt. She adjusted the cervical collar she was wearing because of the mild whiplash she'd gotten either in the crash or the scotch broom or both. She decided to try listing the pluses and minuses. On the plus side, when the crash happened, her cell phone had come flying out from wherever it had gotten lodged when they went through the field. So, at least she hadn't lost her phone.

She thought for a couple of minutes. That was pretty much it for the pluses.

On the minus side, her almost-ex could die, and she'd probably be in jail, despite what Tally thought. *They might even get me for first degree murder. Everybody knew I hated his guts, they'll probably say I've been planning it for months. I mean, my god, the police have impounded Logan's car. They're probably going over it with a fine-toothed comb. Oh god, I can just hear the prosecutor describing how I sabotaged the brake, knowing my almost-ex would be walking to Josephine's office at that exact time, and how I did a horrible job of teaching Mrs. Hanama to drive all these months, so that there was no way she would be able to stop the car...*

She couldn't imagine a good outcome.

She dug behind the cushions until she felt the phone. But as she pulled it from behind the cushion, an image of it wedged behind the brake flashed across her mind. *Oh god, is that why it didn't stop us?*

Her phone rang in her hand. It was Tally calling back. "Look, Sal, I don't want to alarm you, but I really think you should get ahold of your lawyer, for both you and Logan's sake."

"What...?" Sally didn't like the sound of this. There was a frightening urgency in her sister's voice.

"Well, after I talked to you, I called Jack's mom. She and I have always gotten along, and I just thought I'd give it a shot. I, you know, expressed my concern, and it sounded like she needed someone to talk to, so I was able to find out a few things."

Sally sat up and took notice. "What? What?"

"Apparently Jack woke up, and is basically not in such bad shape, except for bumps and bruises, and a badly broken leg, which he was just going into surgery for."

"Oh god, he's okay! I am so relieved. When you started, I thought you had bad news, but now—"

"Wait a minute, Sal, there's more. She said he's threatened to sue you and Logan for everything he can get."

"But, like you said earlier, he crossed against the light—can he really get anything?

"Well, people sue all the time, even for things that are obviously their fault, and the person getting sued has to get a lawyer and everything, and with Logan having a driving school, it'll prolong the bad publicity, so..."

"Oh god, you're right, Tal. The way Jack operates...I've gotta call Josephine." Sally left another message with Josephine's secretary. She was assured that Josephine wasn't ducking her, and would respond as soon as she could.

She paced around and around the apartment. Getting dizzy, she plopped down in her big comfy chair. As she sat there, she noticed the rain had stopped. She decided to go out on the roof. *Yeah, a little fresh air will help, I'm sure. I think.*

She paced back and forth on the roof. The pacing out there was definitely much more satisfying. When her phone rang, she assumed it was Tally. But she saw that it was Logan. She let it ring, then finally answered.

"Hi."

She waited to hear his voice at the other end. He took his time.

"Hi. Uh, are you doing okay?"

"Not exactly. You?"

"Well, uh, actually things are looking up a little bit. The police are releasing the car tomorrow, now that it looks like your hubby's gonna be okay. "

"Well, that's good, I guess." *What the hell? His stupid car? Wait till he hears he's gonna get sued back to the Stone Age...*

"They said one of the bolts that holds the brake in was sheared off on the underside of the car, so that might have been why the brake didn't work as well as it should have. It might have happened when you guys hit the curb."

"We hit the curb?"

"Yeah, that's part of what stopped you."

How did I not know that? And the bolt. Could Jack have sawed that or something? But she then she remembered the car bumping through the scotch broom...*did we hit a rock?*

"Anyway, it looks like we might get through this."

"Uh, look, I hate to rain on your parade, Logan, but now that my almost-ex is awake, he's threatening to sue for everything he can get."

Silence at the other end. Finally he spoke. "Shit."

"I agree completely." Sally adjusted her neck collar again.

A sigh from the other end. "God, I just get out of one lawsuit to land in another one."

"Yeah, I know the feeling. I haven't even gotten out of divorce court, and he's taking me to civil court. I feel like I'm about to get sued for everything I don't have yet."

"Can husbands sue wives?"

"Not sure." This was a possible bright spot that hadn't occurred to her. *Damn. I have to get ahold of Josephine.*

"Okay, uh, I need to call Josephine. I'll call you back."

"Good luck. I've been trying all day."

"Oh. Okay, I'll let her know that. 'Bye, Sal."

It was beginning to pour rain, literally. Sally ducked back into the apartment. Her neck hurt, she was worried and depressed. She felt completely alone. When she tried to watch TV, there was some guy on a reality show trying to see how many olives he could shove in his mouth in thirty seconds. She turned it off and took a pain pill. She sat on the couch watching the rain come down until she fell into a dark dreamless sleep.

·/·

She awoke to the phone ringing. It was Tally again.

"Tal? What's up? Did you find out any more from Jack's mom?"

"No, actually...I...uh..."

"What? Tal? Is it that bad?"

"No, Sal, Really, it's not. It's just that I'm still kind of in shock. Actually, it's good."

"Good? I could use some good news. What?"

"Well, Jack called."

"From the hospital?"

"Yeah. He sounded really weird, so I'm not exactly sure whether to believe this, but if it's true, it's good.

"I'm in the mood for 'good,' tell me—I don't even care if it's true or not."

"Well, he sounded kind of dreamy, and he said he'd had an experience that has changed his life."

"What, Jack got religion or something?" Sally plopped down on the couch. She wasn't sure whether this was good or bad.

"Well, not exactly, but sort of, I guess..."

"Tally, will you just flipping spit it out? What happened?"

"From what he said, I guess, he had a near death experience of some kind. He said it was when he was in the operating room, and he floated around the room and looked down on everyone, you know, just like you always hear about."

Sally ran her fingers through her hair and tried to think. Was this good? If it was 'near' death, that meant he was still alive—well, of course he was still alive, he'd called Tally—but...

"Anyway, he said he's forgiven you, and he wants to get the divorce over with, so you can both get on with your lives. And get this, Sal, he wants to give you your fair share."

"He said that?"

"He said 'fair share.'"

"I wonder what his idea of my fair share is."

"I don't know, Sally, but I think this is good, don't you?"

"Yeah, yeah, it sounds like it. I just hope it isn't one of his tricks."

"I don't think so, Sal. I mean, he sounded sincere."

"He's good at that. But let's hope he really is this time."

After talking with Tally, Sally paced around and around again. She was excited, apprehensive, confused...She knew she should be ecstatic. *But what if he's just getting ready to pull the rug out from under me for the hundredth time? How am I supposed to believe he had some deeply spiritual experience? Jack? Really?*

The next call was Josephine.

"Apparently your husband has had a change of heart."

"He called you, too?"

"His lawyer called. I'll have some things for you to sign in the next few days, it sounds like."

"So, this is for real?"

"His lawyer seemed to think so."

"Wow."

"Wow, indeed. Your wish might finally come true."

When Sally finished her conversation with Josephine, she was completely dazed. She stared out at the spring rain, the tiny drops falling straight down, while the sun shone through. The dreamy quality of the scene perfectly reflected her mood. After a few minutes, she stood up. She needed to convince herself this was all real, and for some reason that seemed to involve Logan.

•/•

A little while later, she strolled into the office, trying to seem nonchalant. Gwelda glanced up from her phone and her thumbs stopped in their tracks.

"Is Logan around?" He wasn't at his desk. Sally looked around, then hoped he was just in the restroom. Despite the situation, she wanted to see him, and believed they would have some magical moment where everything between them would be fine again, regardless of everything around them.

"Yeah, I think he's out back doing something on one of the cars. Um, I haven't seen you since the crash...Are you, like...okay and everything?"

"Yeah, yeah, I got a massage and my neck's a lot better now. Nothing showed up on the x-rays right after the crash, so it was probably just strained muscles."

"Um, I guess Logan and Dave think it was my bad about the brake, but honestly I don't remember anybody telling me it needed work. I went through my stack of car trouble reports, and..."

"Gwelda, don't worry about it. I'm pretty sure it was just one of those things. Not everything in life is one person's fault." Hearing herself say that made Sally think about her marriage. *Yeah. I guess I could give him a break, too.*

Gwelda looked directly at Sally for a moment, with an expression as if she were seeing her for the first time. "Um, thanks, Sally. It seems like everybody's been so mad at me, I just..." Gwelda's lower lip quivered, and Sally realized she was near tears.

"It wasn't really fair for the guys to take it out on you. I think it was just that there was nobody else around. You know how guys are."

Gwelda nodded, rolling her eyes. She looked at Sally for a long moment and a quick almost smile formed before it disappeared just as quickly. Sally took it to mean something like "Thanks."

"I'll go see if I can find Logan." Sally headed out the door to go around to the back parking lot. Logan was replacing the wiper blades on his car, and looked up as she approached.

"So, you haven't gotten the car back yet?"

"Dave's going to pick it up."

"How bad's the damage? I didn't really see at the time. They kind of whisked me off to the hospital for x-rays and…"

"It's not that bad—the hood mostly." He continued to concentrate on tinkering with the wiper blade, although it looked to her like the job was pretty much done.

"Logan…" She couldn't seem to think of a follow up. "Logan." She kept thinking that if she started off with his name, the rest would follow. But it didn't.

"Yes…Yes?" He responded each time, without looking up. Finally when she didn't continue, he looked directly at her. "Sal, I don't think it was your fault, you know."

"Actually, I think it may—" Sally's phone buzzed in her pocket. It was Josephine's office. Her secretary wanted to know if Sally could come in at one o'clock. "Uh, yeah, sure." Sally shoved her phone in her pocket. She didn't feel able to finish the sentence she had started. She didn't really know if it was her fault, and what good would it do anyway to take the blame, unless it really was. If it was her fault, it was the company's fault, and she would just be making things worse for Logan. "I have good news. Jack woke up, and he's in a very generous mood. He's not going to sue, after all. He had some kind of near death experience."

"Really? When did you find this out?"

"This morning. He called Tally, for some reason. That's why Josephine just called to have me come in today. Jack wants to get the divorce over with and even give me a fair settlement." Somehow saying it out loud to Logan did make it seem like it might really happen.

144

"Sal, that's awesome! I'm really happy for you." Then his expression darkened. "So I guess that means you'll be..." His voice trailed off as he looked down and started to fiddle with the wiper blade again.

"I'll be going to school, Logan, but school's expensive these days, I'm pretty sure I'll still need to work here at least a few hours a week."

He instantly brightened. "You really think so?"

"Yeah, sure, I mean who else is gonna finish Mrs. Hanama's lessons?" She laughed, and he joined in.

"Not me!' He put up both hands as if to fend off the possibility. "How's she doing, anyway? I talked to her the day after, but I suppose I should check on her again." There was genuine concern in his voice.

He's really a sweet, caring guy, even if he's a little clumsy sometimes. "I really need to call her, too. It wasn't really her fault, but I'm sure she thinks so. And her husband is probably not being any help."

"Yeah. Maybe Robert's giving her some hugs."

I could use some of those myself...

It was like he read her mind. He lifted his arms up just a bit, just enough to suggest a hug if she wanted it, but he could still have pretended he was just shrugging or getting a kink out of his neck, if needed. She seized the opportunity, and fell into his arms. It felt so good, was such a relief that the dam broke, and everything that had been building for the past few days and maybe more, came flooding out. The tears seemed to have a life of their own, and try as she did to stop them, they kept flowing well past the point that she thought might be reasonable to cry on one's boss's shoulder.

"It's okay, Sal, things are looking good for you now, what's this all about? Everything's going your way." He held her and patted her back, and whatever he said didn't matter, just the sound of his voice made her begin to feel better.

•/•

Later Sally sat in Josephine's office looking over the settlement offer. All she had to do was give it her blessing, and it could all be over. Still, what was there didn't seem like much for twelve long years together. She thought back to where she'd been, and who she'd been when she met Jack.

"Don't overthink it, dear." Josephine broke into her reverie. "I know it's probably not all that you hoped for, but he's going to have some medical bills to pay, and there may not have been as much to split as you were hoping, in the first place."

"I know, I just…" Sally wasn't even sure how she had been planning to finish that sentence.

"Let me give you a thought, Sally. The two most important skills to learn if you want to be happy in life are negotiation, and rationalization."

Sally tried not to look at her lawyer as if she was completely flipping senile, but she was pretty sure (1) that she was looking at her lawyer that way, and (2) that her lawyer was completely flipping senile. Negotiation and rationalization were not goals to be aspired to. She knew that much even at her age, and hoped she would have a lot more wisdom than that to impart by the time she was Josephine's age.

"You negotiate the best situation you can for yourself, and then rationalize each day that it's just right for you. You relax into it, enjoy it. You don't fight it."

"You just settle? That doesn't seem right."

"Do you want to be right more than you want to be happy?"

"I want both."

"Well then, do the right thing for yourself each time you have an opportunity: negotiate the best situation. Then weed out unwanted, unnecessary thoughts. That's one definition of rationalizing, you know. You want to be an English teacher, right?"

"Y-yes." *Dammit, it sounds like Josephine knows what she's talking about again.*

"So, understand the meaning of the word. Weed out stray thoughts like: Could this have been better? Did I get shafted? Grab what you got and say, boy, this is great, then enjoy it. If everybody else thinks you should have gotten more, why should you care? You'll be too busy making the most of what you did get."

Sally gazed at Josephine, trying to absorb all that she'd just said.

"Do you really want to burn more time on this, Sally? As for me, I have some other things to attend to, so I'll leave you alone with these papers, and some time to decide." Josephine got up from her desk and walked out of the office.

Sally tried to think, but kept hearing the voices of her sister, and her mother, and everyone she'd ever known, it seemed, telling her not to settle for less, that she'd regret it forever, that she should stick to her guns, when weirdly the voice of her father chimed in, "Sally, honey, do you even know what 'stick to your guns' means? I mean really, sweetie, we're sword people."

Sally grabbed a pen off the desk, signed her name, and left.

•/•

"You've pretty much calmed down, then?" Sally was talking to Mrs. Hanama the next day. She wanted to bring up the lotto ticket, but didn't want to be tacky. Now wasn't the time. They were having old-fashioned malts at the bowling alley where Robert worked. "God, this is delicious, Murieta. I'm so glad you suggested it."

"I know, they make me feel better, always." Mrs. Hanama stirred her malt with the straw, then took a big sip.

"And look, whatever Mr. Hanama says about your driving, this was not your fault. It was all very confusing, you couldn't even see Jack, and anyway, he ran across against the light."

"Robert have been saying he'll take me driving next week if I want."

"You should go, Murieta. You shouldn't give up." Sally could hardly believe the words that just seemed to be falling out of her mouth. Was she really telling Mrs. Hanama to get behind the wheel of a car again?

"I think my cousin will give you one quarter of her ticket. She's saying that's two thousand, and that's enough, since she has the ticket, you don't."

"Dollars? Two thousand dollars?"

"That's what she's saying."

The big winner still hadn't turned up, and if they never did, Sally would always wonder, she was sure, if half of that ticket was at the bottom of her shredder. *Weed out unwanted thoughts. Things happen for a reason.* Sally started to laugh. "Wow. That's great, Murieta. Thanks."

She checked her watch, then sucked down the last of her malt. "I should get going, I've got a lot to do. I've got to look into getting registered for school, for one thing. Do you need a ride?"

"No thanks, Robert will."

Sally headed out the door, waving to both Mrs. Hanama and Robert. She was pretty sure it was only a temporary goodbye.

As she drove out of the parking lot she saw a figure standing at the bus stop across the street. There was something very familiar...big goggley sun glasses, dark grey hooded jacket, and mid-length grey skirt...but somehow as different as it was familiar. The Grim Reaper? Wait. No, that couldn't be her, dressed like that. Sally dismissed the thought from her mind, and images of Logan quickly displaced it.

Logan. How to proceed with Logan. She decided she needed some flowers to help her think. She stopped at a store and picked up a couple of bouquets, grabbing a scratch ticket on a whim.

At her little kitchen table, arranging the flowers, she mused about her future, and Logan's place in it. The scratch ticket lay on the table, and she picked it up. As she scratched it off with her fingernail, she got more and more excited. It turned out to be a $50 winner. Nice.

It felt like an omen. She decided to call Logan.

"Hi. What's up, Sal?"

"Well, I signed off on my divorce settlement yesterday."

"Wow. Big step. So...do you want to celebrate? Or are we still on hold, because I'm still gonna be your boss?"

"Well, I was thinking you'll just be my part-time boss, so maybe you could be a part time boyfriend, too?"

"Hey, I'd work overtime on that."

"Funny, Logan. Anyway, I think we need to negotiate some rules."

"Talk it over at dinner?"

"Sure."

"Seven o'clock, Señor Szechuan's?"

"It's a date."

Logan let out an audible breath. "Wow. She said 'date.'"

"Yeah...she did." Sally couldn't help marveling with him. "By the way—"

"What?" He sounded a little paranoid, like her "by the way" might be followed by "I was just kidding about dinner."

"You might want to wear your hardhat—I hear there's a danger of falling piñatas."

He was laughing as their conversation ended.

She put the last flower into the bouquet. She stepped back. It looked...no...she needed to move that one daffodil...as she moved it, a tulip slipped out of place. She put it back in the same place, stopped for a moment and took a deep breath. She put the daffodil where it had been to begin with, then stepped back again. "Perfect," she said quietly to herself. "It was already perfect."

And maybe after our dinner negotiation, Logan and I can do a little rationalizing...at his place."

.⁄. .⁄. .⁄.

Margo E. Peterson

About the Author

Margo Peterson comes by her knowledge of driving instruction honestly. She has worked in driver education in the Pacific Northwest since 1996, owning a driving school for over 12 years. After selling her school she has continued to work part time as an instructor for another company.

Her patience, a crucial quality in this business, stems from her sense of humor, which also stood her in good stead when raising her two children. Now that she is semi-retired, she spends her spare time with her granddaughter, or gardening, and hopes to again do some drawing and painting.